PROMISE

of

JESSICA WOOD

This book is a work of fiction. Names, characters, places, and incidents either are the product of the author's imagination or are used fictitiously. Any resemblance to actual persons, living or dead, events, or locales is entirely coincidental.

ISBN-13: 978-1507877494

ISBN-10: 1507877498

First Edition: April 2015

Also by Jessica Wood

Emma's Story Series

- *A Night to Forget* – Book One
- *The Day to Remember* – Book Two
- *Emma's Story* Box Set – Contains Book One & Book Two

The Heartbreaker Series

This is an *Emma's Story* spin-off series featuring Damian Castillo, a supporting character in *The Day to Remember*. This is a standalone series and does not need to be read with *Emma's Story* series.

- *Damian* – Book One
- *The Heartbreaker* – Prequel Novella to *DAMIAN* – can be read before or after *Damian*.
- *Taming Damian* – Book Two

- *The Heartbreaker Box Set* – Contains all three books.

The Chase Series

This is a standalone series with cameo appearances from Damian Castillo (*The Heartbreaker series*).

- *The Chase, Vol. 1*
- *The Chase, Vol. 2*
- *The Chase, Vol. 3*
- *The Chase, Vol. 4*
- *The Chase: The Complete Series Box Set* – Contains All Four Volumes

Oblivion

This is a standalone full-length book unrelated to other series by Jessica Wood.

- *Oblivion*

Promises Series

This is a standalone series unrelated to other series by Jessica Wood.

- *Promise to Marry* – Book One
- *Promise to Keep* – Book Two
- *Promise of Forever* – Book Three

***

Pre-Orders Currently Available

- *Contracted Love* – June 30, 2015

PROMISE

of

"Forever is composed of nows."

Emily Dickinson

Prologue

CHLOE

People always say that when you're about to die, your life seems to flash before your eyes. I'd never thought too much about what that'd be like until it actually happened to me.

During the last few seconds before the car crashed through the wooden railing and propelled me off the edge of the bridge, time seemed to somehow slow down around me. Those precious seconds seemed to stretch on for a lifetime as images of my past came into focus—one after another—like a continuous stream of clips captured from the various important moments in my life.

Inevitably, Jackson appeared in almost all of them. My heart broke a little more each time he entered my mind. Growing up, he had always been the good in my life, the light at the end of the tunnel, the hope to get me through the hard times. And after nine years apart, I thought I finally had my best friend back. I thought we could finally get back to how things were between us. I thought we finally had a chance to be together.

I was wrong.

After all that'd happened, our love wasn't meant to be. No matter what we did, we couldn't avoid what we couldn't change: our past and who we were. The heavy weight of loss pressed against my chest as I tried to accept this reality. We could never go on that first date tonight. We could never be anything but friends—siblings. We could never keep our promise to marry each other.

But maybe I shouldn't be surprised. Maybe I should have seen it coming. After all, my life had been filled with broken promises since as early as I could remember. When I was young, it had been the promises my mom made to me. Her promise to stop drinking and popping pills. Her promise to get better so we could live together like a family. Her promise that she'd be around to take care of me and be there whenever I needed her. Yet in the end, none of those promises were kept.

So shouldn't I be used to the let-down of unfulfilled promises? Shouldn't I be numbed to the feelings of heartache and despair? Shouldn't I come to expect that the promises I held most dear to my heart would inextricably be the ones that would be left unfulfilled?

Then why had I held on to the hope that Jackson's promise to marry me would be anything different? Why had I ever thought it would be one promise that wouldn't be broken?

As the impact of the car slammed against the surface of the steel-like waters, my body jerked forward like a limp rag doll against the seatbelt that held me in place.

But I didn't feel the pain of the crash's impact. All I felt was the numbing, all-consuming pain of my broken heart as the cold darkness of the water welcomed me into her chilling embrace.

Chapter One

JACKSON

I fell back onto my bed with a wide grin on my face. I let out a deep, soothing sigh, feeling a wave of contentment and excitement wash down over my body. I couldn't remember the last time I'd been as happy as I'd been in the last twenty-four hours with Chloe. I drew in a deep inhale of breath, taking in her sweet scent that still lingered on my clothes, instantly fueling my desire to have her back in my arms again.

"Just a few more hours," I said as I closed my eyes and imagined her lying next to me on the bed. When I'd walked her to her front door, I hadn't wanted to say goodbye. I hadn't wanted to walk away from her. I hadn't realized how much I'd missed her these past nine years until I'd finally given in to my feelings yesterday.

Since I was a teenager, I'd dated my fair share of girls, but none of the relationships ever turned into anything serious—I was never able to commit to a girl. I'd always blamed these failed relationships on external factors—we hadn't been compatible, the timing had been wrong for us, or I had been too busy on my career to be able to make the commitment.

But after just one night with Chloe, I'd realized I was wrong. All my failed relationships hadn't been caused by any external factor. Instead, it'd been an internal one: I'd already given my heart to Chloe years ago and it'd been by her side all along.

As I replayed my memories of yesterday and today in my head, I still couldn't believe the moment

I'd been waiting for since as early as I could remember was finally happening—the moment when I didn't have to pretend I only wanted to be Chloe's best friend, the moment I didn't have to hide my feelings from her or everyone else, the moment we could finally be together.

I reminded myself that I needed to be patient and take things slow. To me, the idea of Chloe being my girlfriend had been a long time coming in my mind. Because of my stubborn pride, we'd lost more than nine years together, and a part of me—the crazy, irrational part—wanted to immediately make up for all the lost time. I wanted to rush to her side and propose to her right now. I wanted us to start our lives together, to begin our happily-ever-after together.

But in reality, this was new territory, and I didn't want to rush Chloe or our relationship. Plus, now that I knew what actually had happened with Chloe in college and the part I'd played in it all, I realized that I didn't deserve the forgiveness and acceptance that she'd offered me so easily. I realized that I didn't deserve her.

For all the times I'd selfishly pushed her away, took her for granted, and misjudged her actions, I knew I needed to make it up to her. I knew I needed to earn her trust and love back.

With a sudden sense of urgency, I leaped out of my bed and strode over to my desk and switched on my laptop. I pulled out my smartphone and pulled up a number.

"Hey, Jackson. What's up? I didn't see you in the office today." I could hear the click-clacking of Nick's keyboard as he answered the phone.

"Hey, Nick. I'm actually still in Philly."

"Oh, I thought you were back yesterday?"

"Yeah, that was the original plan, but something came up and I'll be staying in Philly for at least a few more days. So I'll be working remotely."

"Really? Is anything wrong?"

"No, not at all. Quite the opposite." I laughed at how different and unexpected this past weekend had been. Just last week, I'd thought about canceling on my trip back to Philly. I hadn't wanted to go to Clara and Sam's wedding because Chloe had been the last person I wanted to see.

"Anyway," I continued, "I was calling to ask you for the name of that new restaurant in Philly you were telling me about a few weeks ago. It was the one you took your wife to when you guys were here visiting your in-laws—the nice, intimate one that you said your wife loved?"

"Oh?" I heard the click-clacking of his keyboard stop abruptly as Nick snickered. "Is this about a girl? Did you actually meet someone at the wedding? Is this why you're not back in New York yet? You know I was just teasing you last week about being a bachelor forever, right? I wasn't serious when I dared you to meet someone you can be serious with at the wedding."

I laughed. "Yes, it is about a girl, but no, this has nothing to do with your dare. I've had my eyes on this girl for over twenty years."

"What? No way." Nick chuckled, thinking I was playing with him.

"I'm serious." I smiled to myself at how incredible it was that Chloe and I finally found each other again.

"That doesn't even make sense, though. You're Jackson Pierce—the forever bachelor. Since as long as I've known you, you've never mentioned being interested in a girl for longer than a few months. Twenty years?"

"It's a long story, and I'll tell you about it sometime. But I need to get going, so can you tell me the name of the restaurant?"

"All right, but you owe me a story when you get back into the office." He laughed as I heard the sound of his keyboard start up again. "Okay, found it. It's Ela in the Queen Village neighborhood in Philly."

As soon as I hung up on Nick, I called Ela and made reservations for tonight. I also called the florist to pre-order a special bouquet of Chloe's favorite flowers. I wanted tonight to be special. I wanted Chloe to know how much she meant to me.

After I made all the arrangements for tonight, I jumped into the shower to get ready. As much as a part of me didn't want to wash off the smell and memory of her from my skin, I wanted to look good tonight for our first date. My stomach flipped with anticipation at the thought—it was *finally* going to happen.

By the time I got out of the shower, I was filled to the brim with nervous excitement. I'd spent the last twenty minutes in the shower playing various scenarios of what would happen tonight on our date. I'd imagined how beautiful she would look as she smiled at me—that smile that was sure to be the end of me. I'd imagined the different ways I'd try to sneak in an extra kiss from her at every chance I could. I'd imagined how cute she'd be when she playfully punched me on my chest after I teased her about something.

I looked over at my alarm clock on my nightstand and groaned. There were still four more hours to kill before I was supposed to pick Chloe up from her place. There was so much pent-up nervous energy swirling inside me, I started pacing my room, wondering if I could really wait another four hours.

I strode over to my window that faced her house and glanced over at the window to her bedroom. I smiled and wondered what she was doing right now. *Is she as happy as I am right now? Is she nervous about tonight like I am? Does she miss me already, too?*

"Maybe I could see if she wants to meet earlier?" I asked aloud as the idea popped into my head. I reached for my phone and wondered if I should call her and ask.

Just then, I saw the front door to the house swing open and a second later, Chloe stepped out. A wide smile spread across my face as I felt my chest soar at the sight of her. *Did she have the same idea? Is she coming over to see me?*

But my smile quickly disappeared when I saw the bewildered expression on her face. As I watched her sprinting from the house, leaving the front door wide open behind her, I knew that something wasn't right. *What's going on?*

Without missing a beat, something propelled me to run out of my house and catch up to her. But when I got out of the house, I saw that she had already gotten into her car.

"Chloe!" I cried out as I ran across the lawn. But she didn't hear me. Before I was able to get to her, she had already backed out of the driveway, knocking over the recycling bins at the foot of the path, and was speeding down the block.

My stomach lurched as a wave of worry hit me. By the way her car swerved, I knew with certainty that something was really wrong. I rushed back up my own driveway and jumped in my rental car. I turned onto the street as I saw Chloe's car round the corner.

I pulled out my phone and dialed her number. Her phone started ringing but she didn't pick up. When I was sent to her voicemail, I hung up and called her again.

"Pick up, Clo!" I could hear the panic in my voice as I felt nerves gnaw against my insides. Is she ignoring me? Or is her phone on silent? Or did she leave her phone behind at the house?

I must have taken the wrong turn after rounding the corner on my block because I didn't see her car. After several blocks and turns, I finally saw her car driving erratically down the block from me. I started honking my horn at her, hoping to get her attention, hoping if she saw me, she'd come to her senses and slow down or pull over to tell me what happened.

But she didn't pull over. She didn't slow down. It was as if she couldn't hear me. It didn't take long for me to catch up to her. I continued to honk at her as I approached her car from behind.

It was no use. She still didn't stop or slow down. I felt completely powerless as I continued to honk at her while trying to call her phone. As my heart pounded violently against my chest, I knew I needed to get her attention.

I rolled down my passenger-side window and tried to drive my car up next to hers.

"Clo!" I screamed out at her. "Stop the car!"

But she didn't seem to notice me. There was a dazed gleam in her eyes and I could tell she was crying.

Suddenly, my chest tightened as I saw her car abruptly swerve to the right, just as we approached the bridge overlooking the lake.

"No!" I yelled out when I watched in horror as her car crashed through the wooden railing and hurled off the edge.

I slammed on my brakes and pulled my car to the side of the road. Pushing my door open, I leaped out of the car and ran to the edge of the bridge. Panic and shock nearly paralyzed me as I leaned over the railing to look for Chloe's car. I spotted the back half of her silver Volkswagen Beetle jetting up from the water. But there was no sign of her. A lump developed in my throat, knowing that she was completely submerged underwater.

Adrenaline rushed through me as I raced down the slope of the hill that led down to the lake. I could hear several on-lookers calling out to me, but my mind was too frantic to register anything they were saying. There was only one thought I could focus on and one thought that consumed every fiber of my being: I had to save Chloe.

By the time I reached the edge of the lake, I'd already kicked off my sneakers and ripped off my shirt. Without missing a step, I pulled off my jeans and dove into the bitter-cold water. I swam toward the car as fast as my body could take me. When I reached it, I drew in a deep breath of air before plunging under the icy water, swimming toward the front of the car.

I tried to remain calm and forced myself to focus on the task at hand and to not think about Chloe in pain. But any false sense of calm I'd managed to muster immediately abandoned me the second I reached the front of the car—the second I saw her. She was floating lifelessly inside the car, her long, dark chestnut hair swaying with the undercurrent as it hid her face from me.

Clo! I wanted to scream out to her. I tried to pound against the window, but quickly realized I wouldn't be able to break through it. I reached for the car door handle, and to my surprise, it was unlocked. I pulled against the handle, but the door only opened slightly against the pressure of the water. With some force, I finally pulled opened the car door and pulled myself inside. As soon as I unbuckled the seatbelt from around her, I pulled her limp body out of the car and swam as hard as I could toward the surface of the water.

By the time I pulled Chloe to land, the ambulance had already arrived at the scene. Several EMTs rushed to my side as I tried to perform CPR on Chloe.

"Come on, Clo! Breathe!" I begged as I performed compressions against her chest.

"Sir," said one of the EMTs who rushed in front of me, "please step aside so we can take over."

I reluctantly pulled away from Chloe as I watched the EMTs hover over her body, promptly placing her on a stretcher while placing an oxygen mask over her face.

"Her pulse is weak, but there," one EMT said.

"She may have sustained some head trauma," another EMT announced.

Their words felt like knives through my chest as I tried to mentally process what had just happened. Lost for words, I followed the EMTs up the hill to the road, my eyes never leaving Chloe's motionless body.

Once they reached the road, they transferred her to a gurney and pushed her toward the ambulance. Before they rolled the gurney up into the back of the ambulance, I reached over, grabbed Chloe's cold hand and squeezed it.

"Clo, you'll be okay. I *know* you'll be okay."

But she didn't respond.

After she was secured in the ambulance, one of the EMTs looked over at me expectantly. "Sir, are you a family member?"

"I'm…I'm her boyfriend," I finally managed to croak out.

He gave me an understanding nod. "Okay. We'll need you to follow us and meet us at the hospital and provide us with her information. Also, if possible, could you inform her family that we're taking her to the Chester County Hospital?"

"Yeah," I responded in a low voice. "Will she be okay?"

"I'm sorry, I don't know, but we'll do everything we can to save her."

Without another word, the EMT jumped into the back of the ambulance and pulled the back door closed.

And just like that, I watched in silence as the ambulance's sirens came to life and the flashing red vehicle sped off down the street, taking Chloe away from me.

Save her? I echoed the EMT's words in my head as I headed toward my car. *But she can't...she just can't. I can't lose her now.*

Chapter Two

CHLOE

I couldn't remember how I got there, or why I was there, or even what I'd been doing before that very moment, but there I was, standing in a long, narrow hallway that seemed to stretch on in front of me with no end in sight. The bright florescent lights overhead made the stark-white walls look sterile and unwelcoming around me.

There were doors running along both sides of me. As I started to walk down the hallway, I passed a few. They were all closed, but for some reason, I knew they weren't locked. Every door looked identical—white, like the walls, with only the thin outline of the doors' edges and the shiny brass knobs setting them apart from the walls. There were no signs, numbers, or words on any of the doors, and no way to distinguish one door from the next.

Wondering what or where the doors led me to, I reached for the doorknob of the door that was closest to me. But I didn't turn the knob. I felt hesitant to open the door. Now that I stood only inches from the doorframe, my ears picked up a faint sound over the steady buzzing of the florescent lights. It was coming from the other side of the door. I inched closer and pressed my ears gently against the white paint of the door. The sound was louder now. It was a soft steady beeping.

What is that? I wondered as I pressed my ear harder against the door. I thought about reaching for the doorknob again and opening the door to find out, but I stopped myself. It was almost as if some force held me back, like an invisible barrier that prevented me from moving forward. My curiosity about the beeping on the other side of the door wasn't enough to overcome this barrier.

I was just about to move away from the door and walk away when the sound of a man's voice from the other side of the door stopped me.

"It's all my fault that she's lying here."

Even though his voice was muffled by the door between us, I could hear him clearly. There was something familiar about this voice, almost like I'd heard it before. Something stirred inside me—was it a memory? No, it was a feeling. Warmth and happiness, like home. I tried to think through the fog that filled my thoughts, to try to figure out why I was suddenly feeling nostalgic.

"I could have prevented this," the voice continued. "I should have caught up to her faster and forced her to stop before..." The man trailed off, never finishing the rest of the sentence.

I wasn't sure what or who he was talking about, but from the anguish that seemed to seep into his every word, my interest was piqued. I decided to stay by the door a little longer before moving on and leaned my ear against the door a little more.

"Sweetie, please don't think like that," an elderly female voice responded. "This isn't your fault. You did the best you could."

"No, not my best." The man's voice was strained and I wondered why he sounded so mad. *He can't be mad at this woman, can he?*

"Betty's right," an elderly male voice said. "I know you're upset, but don't beat yourself up like this. You need to stay strong for her. None of us really know what happened earlier today or why she left the house so abruptly. We were in the kitchen and didn't even know she left the house until we heard her cellphone ring non-stop in the living room. We knew she had been upstairs at the time so we called out to her to tell her that her phone was ringing. When she didn't respond, I went to go look for her. That's when I saw the front door wide open and her car gone."

"I should have been there for her," the first voice I'd heard said in frustration. "I saw her face before she…she looked really upset. She looked like she'd been crying."

I could tell by the way he talked about this woman that he loved and cared deeply for her. I wondered what had happened to her. Maybe this man had an argument with her. Maybe he'd made her cry and she left him. I shook my head and sympathized with him. *If only she was here to hear the pain and regret in his voice, she would certainly forgive him and take him back, wouldn't she?*

"Poor child," the woman said with a sigh. "I really wish I knew what made her so upset. I just don't know what I'd do if anything were to happen to her. I told Judy I'd take care of her daughter." The woman's last few words came out like sobs.

"She'll be okay, Betty," the older man reassured. "She's always been so strong. She'll pull through this.

Let's all just stay positive. The doctor said they're probably moving her out of the ICU tonight and into one of the regular hospital rooms. From the scans, her head injuries aren't as severe as the doctors first thought."

"But why isn't she waking up, then?" the woman asked. I could hear the fear in her voice.

"Honey, remember what the doctors said. It's just a matter of time," the older man reassured. "She's responding to stimuli, so she's not comatose. Right now we just have to wait until she wakes up. It's up to her now, and Chloe's a fighter. I believe in her, don't you?"

"I do," the younger man answered instead. "I believe in her. She's stronger than anyone I know." There was so much conviction in his voice that for some reason, I was touched by his words.

From what I could gather from their conversation, I knew I'd been wrong earlier. This man didn't have an argument with this woman named Chloe. It sounded like something had happened to her.

I wondered if she was okay. *I hope so,* I thought to myself. *I hope, for his sake, this Chloe will be okay.* A wave of sadness filled me at the thought of this man in pain and I wiped away a tear that was running down my face.

"You're right, Jackson," the woman agreed. "I believe in her."

When I heard the man's name, something stirred inside me again. I blinked, trying to understand what it was that I was feeling.

"Well, it's getting late," the man named Jackson said. "Aunt Betty, you just got back from the hospital today. I know it's been a long day for both of you. Why don't you guys head home and get some rest? I'll stay with her and keep her company. I'll call you guys if there are any changes."

"That's probably a good idea. Betty, you're still on some medication, and the doctor said it can cause some drowsiness. We can come back early tomorrow morning."

"Okay," the woman said reluctantly. "Are you sure you're okay staying here by yourself for the rest of the night, Jackson? You haven't eaten dinner yet."

"Don't worry about me, really. I'll just get some food from the cafeteria or get some delivered here."

"You've always been such a good kid, Jackson," the woman said affectionately. "I'm so happy to hear that you guys finally worked out your problems."

"Yeah, me too," Jackson agreed. "Of course, I have to thank you for the needed kick-in-the-butt for me to realize what an idiot I'd been."

"Sometimes we all need someone else to give us a nudge to be able to see things clearly."

"Here's your jacket, Betty," the older man said. I heard some rustling. "Should we get going?"

"Yeah."

"Thanks for staying with her tonight," the man said. "Chloe's really lucky to have you as a friend, Jackson."

"Thanks, Uncle Tom."

"Bye, Jackson," the woman said.

"Bye, guys. Have a good night."

As I heard another door open and close, my mind was swirling through the dense fog that blanketed my thoughts.

I wasn't sure why, but my thoughts couldn't seem to let go of this man's name.

Jackson.

Jackson.

Jackson.

As the name echoed in my mind, something unexpected happened. Without thinking, I reached for the doorknob and pushed open the door. When the door opened in front of me, it was like a switch inside my head had suddenly been flipped on, lifting the barrier that separated me from all the memories I hadn't known existed. One memory after another started flooding into my mind. Within seconds, I remembered everything—every precious memory I'd held dear to my heart and every painful memory I'd wanted so desperately to forget.

I was the Chloe these voices had been talking about. And that voice I'd been drawn to, the man I'd felt sorry for just moments before, was Jackson—my Jackson.

No, not your *Jackson, never your Jackson,* a voice in my mind reminded me as one of my most painful memories emerged to the forefront of my thoughts.

I looked into the small room the door led into. It was white and empty with no windows or fixtures. There were also no other doors besides the one I'd just opened.

Where did they go? How did they leave this room? But didn't Jax say he'd stay with me? Had he changed his mind?

With so many questions swimming around in my head, I wasn't sure what was going on. As I took a small step into the room, I tried to remember how I got there. I thought back to the conversation I'd heard Jackson having with Aunt Betty and Uncle Tom moments ago. I remembered them mentioning doctors and being in the ICU.

Am I at a hospital? I looked around the window-less room and then back out into the endless white hallway. But this doesn't make sense. This isn't what a hospital looks like. If it is a hospital, then there should be people—doctors, nurses, patients, visitors. But there is no one here. No one besides me.

Then I felt something—a warm tingle on top of my right hand. *That kind of felt like a hand!* I looked down, expecting to see the source of the feeling. But to my surprise, there was nothing on top of my hand.

Am I losing it? There's no one here. How can there be a hand if there's no one here? I must have imagined the hand on mine, right?

Suddenly—almost as if to prove me wrong—I felt a hand firmly squeeze mine, which sent a ripple of warm tingles to pass through my body.

How can something be imaginary if it feels so real? I asked myself, wondering what this all meant.

I felt completely confused and disoriented. I knew I was missing something—something big that was staring me right in the face. I felt like I could figure out the answers to my questions if I could just push away the fog that blurred my thoughts. I felt like I knew what was going on, but somehow, my mind was scattered about like an unfinished box of puzzle pieces.

"Clo." His familiar, soothing voice broke through the silence, startling me out of my thoughts.

I whipped around to look behind me, expecting him to be standing there at the entrance of the door.

But he wasn't there.

I turned back to face the empty room. Nothing.

Maybe I'm hearing things? Jax isn't here.

"I need you to fight through this, Clo," came his voice again.

I didn't have to look around again to know he wasn't in the room. His voice seemed to resonate through the emptiness of the room, through the walls, and throughout the hallway, almost as if he were on a PA system that covered the entire facility.

"You're a fighter."

Jackson's words reminded me of something Uncle Tom had said earlier. "Right now we just have to wait until she wakes up. It's up to her now, and Chloe's a fighter."

Am I still asleep? Am I unconscious? I looked around my surroundings again. *This place doesn't seem like it's real. And I don't remember coming here.* I tried again to think of the last thing I was doing before I found myself in the white hallway.

I was in my car…I just found John's letters to my mom…I was upset…then I lost control of the wheel… Then it hit me. I drove off the bridge and into the lake!

"You need to wake up, Clo. I still have so many questions for you. Like why did you leave your house so abruptly? Why were you upset? Why didn't you pull over when I was behind your car? Why did you ignore me when I was honking at you to stop?" His questions came out in waves of grief.

He was behind me? I took in his words, wondering if I understood them correctly. I tried to think back to the minutes leading up to the moment the car crashed through the bridge railing. I couldn't remember seeing him behind me or hearing any honking. I remembered that I'd been a wreck when I ran out of the house. The radio had been on when I was driving and I had been crying so hard, I could barely see a thing on the road.

I heard him let out a heavy sigh through his mouth and I felt my chest tighten at the thought of him in so much agony.

I *didn't mean to swerve off the bridge! I didn't realize you were behind me*, I wanted to scream out. But I knew he wouldn't be able to hear me. By then, it was clear to me that somehow I hadn't died in the lake that day. I was lying in a hospital bed, unconscious. From what Uncle Tom had said earlier, whether or not I was going to wake up was now up to me. I wondered if that was true. More importantly, I wondered if I really wanted to wake up.

"Please just wake up, Clo," Jackson said, almost as if he were objecting to my last thought. "We're supposed to be on our first date right now. We're supposed to be happy right now." I heard him sigh again, this time low and drawn out. "You wanna hear about the night I had planned out for us tonight? It was going to be perfect. I was going to pick you up early because I couldn't wait to see you. Of course, you had no objections to that because you were dying to see me, too." He gave a little chuckle. "I was going to have a large bouquet of tulips for you when I picked you up. That would make you smile, which was going to make me smile because I love the way you look when you smile like that. We were going to have a romantic dinner at this amazing restaurant called Ela in the city. We would eat amazing food, drink lots and lots of wine, and lose ourselves in each other's company. Then at some point, our waiter would probably come over to our table and ask us to leave because the restaurant was already closed. After dinner, we would go on a nice, leisurely stroll down South Street. At some point, we would probably stop at one of the bars on that street and grab a small table in a secluded corner. You'd laugh at all my silly jokes that you don't find funny, and I would let you punch me a few times because I know that's one of your favorite pastimes." He chuckled again. "Clo, it would be like how we used to be. Except it'd be better, because now I could kiss you whenever I wanted to—which is like all the time, by the way—and hold you in my arms, and tell you how I feel about you without worrying about how you'd respond."

He paused and I felt him lift my hand with both of his, bringing it up against his lips as he kissed my fingers tenderly. "Tonight was fun, Clo. You looked beautiful and happy. I couldn't have wished for a more perfect date, or a more perfect person to go on this date with."

I could hear the longing and heartache in his voice and it broke my heart. *But this pain is far better than the pain he'd feel if he knew the truth.*

His words were also painful to hear. It was a reminder of everything that was possible between us if things had been different—if we weren't who we were. But I was Chloe and he was Jackson. That wasn't something either one of us could ever change.

I drew in a deep breath and walked back to the doorway of the empty, windowless room.

I turned back and took one last look over my shoulder.

Let me go, Jax, I wished I could say. You deserve a chance to live a happy life—even if I can't be a part of it. Maybe someday you'll be able to forget me. And maybe in another lifetime, we'll find each other again under different circumstances, and fall in love with each other again. But until then, please just let me go.

I stepped back into the stark, white hallway and closed the door behind me. As I stared down the endless corridor before me, I made myself a promise: I would not open any more doors.

Chapter Three

JACKSON

"Tell me a story, Jax," she said in a soft voice. I could tell she was starting to get tired.

"What kind of story?" I chuckled, picturing how cute she probably looked right now lying on her bed with her cellphone to her ear. We'd been talking on the phone for several hours now, and at some point, we'd both moved from our respective couches to our beds, unwilling to be the one to end our call.

"Mmm, any story...maybe something with a happy ending." Her voice drifted in and out and I could hear the pull of sleep overcoming her.

I looked over at the alarm clock sitting on my bedside table and realized it was almost two o'clock in the morning. I groaned to myself, wondering why I'd thought an eight a.m. class this semester was going to be a good idea. It was the start of our second semester of our junior year of college. I was starting to get into the slacker mode as my senior year and graduation loomed ahead. I wondered how often I was going to skip this eight a.m. class.

I yawned and realized I was also getting tired. But I didn't care. Sleep deprivation and some missed classes were worth the trade off—being able to talk to Chloe for hours on end and knowing our friendship was as strong as it'd been in high school. It'd been about a year since our huge fight that morning when she had showed up unexpectedly at my frat house and walked in on me having sex with Amber. After she had driven back to Philadelphia looking upset and hurt, I'd felt guilty about what had happened afterward. But I wasn't sure why. Chloe and I hadn't been in a relationship and she'd made it clear to me that she wasn't interested in me. I wasn't sure why she was upset and why I'd felt guilty about being with Amber. But, nevertheless, the guilt had stayed with me, and had been made worse by the fact that we hardly talked for the rest of that semester. It wasn't until summer break when we were both back home in West Chester that we finally made up.

"Okay, you want a story with a happy ending?" I paused and grinned to myself. "Hmmm, what kind of happy ending?" I tried to stifle a snicker.

"Jax, get your head out of the gutter," she pouted. But she didn't sound upset. She seemed too tired to even bother faking it. "You're such a guy sometimes."

"Well, that's probably because I am a guy, all the time—I mean, in case you forgot," I said with amusement.

"Smart-ass," she shot back. "Fine, I don't want to hear a story anymore. So no happy endings for either of us."

"Aww, really? Breaking a guy's heart here." My sentence broke into a fit of laughter.

"Sometimes you're impossible."

"It's a part of my charm that you find irresistible." I couldn't help but want to flirt with her. Sometimes I found myself forgetting that we were just best friends and nothing else. Sometimes I found myself talking to her like she was my girlfriend. I knew I had to be careful though and not cross the line. I knew she wasn't interested in me like that and the last thing I wanted was to ruin our friendship and lose her because I had made things uncomfortable between us.

"When did I ever tell you that you were irresistible?" She giggled like I'd just told a joke. "Good one, Jax. I think you must have confused me for another girl that you're actually interested in." There was an edge to her voice that I didn't understand.

I smiled. "You've never admitted it out loud, but I know that's what you're thinking," I continued playfully.

"If you say so."

I was sure that she was rolling her eyes at that very moment, or thinking about rolling her eyes if she was too tired to actually do so.

"Jax?" I heard her yawn.

"Yeah, Clo?" I found myself yawning back.

"Promise me—" She yawned again and her words came out slower. "Promise me we'll always be good friends like this."

"I promise, Clo."

"Good," she murmured. "I'd miss you too much if we weren't."

"Me too." My words came out like a whisper.

I could hear her breathing getting deeper. "Should we hang up the phone?" I finally asked.

"No..." she murmured. "Let's stay like this a little longer...I don't want you to go yet..."

"Okay." I smiled and whispered, "Me either."

As I lay there on my bed, feeling the inviting pull of sleep and hearing her soft, deep breathing in my ear, the rest of the world started to drift away around me and all I could feel was her presence. It felt as if the hundreds of miles between us had disappeared and she was there lying next to me in my bed. I closed my eyes and imagined her next to me. She was smiling at me and she looked so beautiful—her soft, pink lips, those rosy cheeks, and her light brown eyes that always had a way of lighting up any room.

"You're falling asleep," I said in a low voice. It came out as a statement but I'd meant it as a question.

"No…" I heard her yawn again. "No…. just one more…" She paused and let out a soft sigh. "…minute...and I'll get up...not time yet..." Then she mumbled something that was completely incoherent and slurred.

"You're cute even when you're not making sense," I whispered into the phone.

She responded with a deep exhale of breath.

As much as I didn't want to end our call and lose the feeling of her presence, the heaviness of my own lids began to overtake my willpower to stay awake.

"Good night, Clo," I whispered into the phone. "Sweet dreams." Sweet dreams of me, I hope, I added to myself. Then I clicked off.

As I drifted off to sleep, I imagined her sleeping peacefully in my arms as I inhaled the sweet smell of her hair. If there comes a day when she's really falling asleep in my arms, I know I wouldn't be able to let her go. That was the last thought I had before I fell asleep.

"Honey?" came a soft voice. Then I felt a hand on my shoulder, and I opened my eyes to see Aunt Betty looking down at me.

I looked over to my left and saw Chloe lying motionless on the hospital bed and reality quickly set in. That had been a dream—a flashback to a moment in time that'd happened almost ten years ago, to a moment in time when Chloe wasn't lying unconscious in a hospital room.

"Sorry, Aunt Betty, I must have drifted off."

"Nothing to apologize for, Jackson. You've been here since she was brought here yesterday. Maybe you should go home and take a nice relaxing shower and get some sleep. I haven't seen you leave her side for longer than a few minutes."

I rubbed the sleep from my eyes. "Nah, it's okay. I took a quick shower here already this morning when Uncle Tom brought over some change of clothes for me and I got a few hours of sleep last night on the bench by the window. I know if I go home and try to sleep, I wouldn't be able to. I'd rather be here for her."

"Okay, dear. Do whatever makes you feel at ease with things."

"Yeah, don't worry about me." I got up from the chair and walked to the private bathroom in the corner of the room. I filled a wash pan with some warm water and grabbed a washcloth.

"What are you doing?" Aunt Betty asked as she watched me with curiosity.

"I'm just wiping her face and arms. I thought maybe if she could feel the warm, wet towel on her skin, it might trigger a response from her. Or at the very least, it'd help her feel refreshed and comfortable."

She nodded with understanding. "I know if she could tell you right now, she'd tell you how much she appreciates everything you're doing for her."

I responded with a small, forced smile. "It's the least I can do right now."

"Well, Tom's pulling the car around and we're going to go home and have some lunch. We'll be back in the afternoon. Just give us a call if you need us to bring you anything, okay?"

"Thanks. I'll let you guys know if anything changes here."

"Thanks, sweetie. Maybe for tonight, we can ask the nurses if they can bring in a cot or something for you to sleep on?" She looked at me with concern. "That bench couldn't have been comfortable last night."

"Yeah, maybe. But really, don't worry. I'll be fine."

"Okay, goodnight, Jackson."

I nodded and waved goodbye.

When Aunt Betty left, I turned my attention to Chloe and gave her a solemn smile.

"Alone at last, huh?" I joked, wishing desperately that she'd respond with a laugh, or an eye-roll, or even a punch aimed at my chest.

I sighed and reached for the washcloth that was soaking in the wash pan and wrung it out.

"I'm here to take care of you, Clo," I said to her as I moved the washcloth gently across her forehead. "I know I should have been around to take care of you during the past nine years. I'm sorry that I wasn't there for you. I hope you will forgive me for that."

I returned the washcloth to the pan, wrung out the excess water, and moved on to her hands. "Clo, you'll be okay. I know you will. Right now, you just have to work hard to open your eyes and wake up, okay?"

After I finished wiping her down, I reached for Chloe's hairbrush I'd asked Uncle Tom to bring over this morning and started to brush her beautiful chestnut-brown hair.

Then I had an idea.

"Okay, so you're not going to like this. You might even hit me for it." I paused for dramatic effect. "But it must be done." I held up the brush. "It's Pippi Longstocking time." I let out a light chuckle as I divided her hair into two parts and tried to remember the time she'd showed me how to braid a pigtail when we were kids.

She didn't respond.

I sighed, but tried to stay upbeat. "Don't be like that and give me the silent treatment." I started to braid one of the pigtails. "You know I don't like when you ignore me. Besides, I've never told you this, but I think you look really cute with pigtails."

When I finished the braid on one side, I moved to the other side of her bed to start on the braid there.

"Okay, in all seriousness, I'm not trying to tease you or make you mad, I just want you to respond to me." I secured a hair-tie around the end of the braid. "I also just want to make you happy. I remember you'd told me once that your favorite moments with your mom were when she would put your hair in pigtails. Those moments were special for you."

I sat down on the chair next to her bed and looked at her, waiting for some sign that she could hear me. I'd been talking to her a lot when we were alone during the past two days. I didn't know what else I could do but to talk to her. It was the only way I could stay sane. It was the only way I could believe things haven't changed. It was the only way I could feel her still here with me. So I needed to continue to talk to her, continue to believe that she could hear me.

"So I had a nice dream about you just now," I continued. "We were still in college and had one of our marathon phone-call sessions. Remember those? When we used to talk on the phone until two or three in the morning? Our ears would be hot and throbbing because we'd have the phone against them for so long." I chuckled. "Good times, huh? I really miss those times together. Don't you?"

I leaned in closer to her. "Can you hear me, Clo? If you can hear me, can you try to wake up? Please?" I shut my eyes and tried to push away the thought of her leaving me.

"I just got you back in my life, I can't lose you now. I promised you when we were kids that I'd always be there for you. But I was an asshole and broke that promise. I fucked up a lot when it came to us, and I know I've hurt you time and time again. It's about time I made it all up to you."

I reached for her hand and kissed it gently. "Please wake up and let me spend the rest of my life making it up to you. Please be okay. Please live." My voice shook with emotion as I dropped my head in despair.

Just then, I thought I felt her fingers twitch in my hands. For a brief second, I froze in place, wondering if I had imagined it out of desperation.

"Clo?" I exclaimed excitedly as I stood from my chair. "It's me. It's Jackson. Can you hear me?" I squeezed her hand. "Can you feel this?"

I held my breath as I watched her carefully, waiting for another sign of movement from her.

When seconds passed and nothing happened, I started to feel the hope and excitement draining from me. And just as I was beginning to think that maybe I had imagined her fingers moving, her eyes fluttered opened and she looked up at me.

"Jax," she managed to say in a weak voice.

Chapter Four

CHLOE

"Clo." He stared down at me with emotions pouring out from the depths of his rich, emerald eyes.

"Jax?" I managed a weak smile as his face came into focus. He looked as handsome as ever as he returned a smile. As I looked into his eyes, there was a nagging ache somewhere deep inside my chest that I couldn't seem to pinpoint.

"Thank God you're finally awake. How are you feeling?" He held onto my hand tightly as he waited expectantly for my response.

"I'm alright, I think."

"Let me tell the nurse and text Aunt Betty that you're up." He raced out of the room but was back in less than a minute. "Aunt Betty and Uncle Tom are on their way back. The nurse will be by in a minute."

"Why am I here? What happened?" My head hurt and I couldn't seem to remember how I'd gotten here. I looked around the room. I noticed the heart monitor screen beside my bed as my nose registered the distinct smell of disinfectant in the air. "Is this a hospital?"

"Yeah. You were in a car accident. Do you remember what happened?" He looked at me with concern.

"A car accident?" I closed my eyes and tried to think through the throbbing headache that made it hard to think.

"Yeah. It was after we got back from the lake. We had plans to go on a date that night. I happened to have been looking out my window when I saw you running out of your house. You got in your car and sped off…"

His words brought images to the forefront of my thoughts. I was in my car. I was crying and could barely focus on the road. I lost control of the wheel and the car crashed through the bridge railing. Then another memory came into focus that sent a chill down my body. I found the letters in the attic.

"I followed you and tried to get your attention with my car, but you didn't seem to hear me—"

"I didn't hear you," I cut in, my voice now distant and flat. I lowered my gaze, unable to bear the pain of looking into his eyes—of seeing the one person I wanted but couldn't have.

"You didn't? But I had followed right behind you for at least two or three blocks and I was honking almost the entire time." He wasn't trying to be argumentative, but I could sense the disbelief in his voice.

"I…I think I had the radio on blast, so I didn't hear you."

There was a pause before he gave a slight nod. "That makes sense." He didn't sound convinced. Then he paused again before continuing. "Clo?"

"Yeah?" I answered reluctantly as I tried to work through my own thoughts about how I was going to tell Jackson about the letters I found.

"D—do you remember if you lost control of your car when you crashed through the bridge railing?"

"I think so." Those last few seconds before I crashed into the water seemed like a distant dream. "It all happened so fast."

"I'm so glad you're safe now." From the corner of my eyes, I saw his chest fall as he let out a deep, silent sigh.

Did he think I drove off the bridge on purpose? The question crossed my mind as I noticed Jackson's body start to relax.

It was then that my mind focused in on the warmth of his hands that had been clasped around mine. My heart broke. I wanted more than anything to be able to enjoy the simple pleasure of his touch. But I knew it was wrong. I knew I couldn't allow myself to enjoy it. I knew I couldn't allow him to touch me this way. As innocent as this gesture was on its own, there was nothing innocent about it when it came to what Jackson and I were to each other and how his touch made me feel—and made me desire.

I pulled my hand out from between his and pretended to brush a loose strand of hair from my face. But when my hand brushed through my hair, I realized it had been braided. I looked down and saw two braids on either side of my shoulders.

"Oh yeah," Jackson said as he followed my gaze, "I should probably warn you…" He trailed off and I could detect a hint of amusement in his voice, which caused me to look up at him. At that moment, my curiosity outweighed my need to distance myself.

Sure enough, there was that devious, boyish grin on his face.

"Warn me about what?" I eyed him suspiciously.

He avoided my gaze and cleared his throat. "Well, while you were asleep, I…umm…I took a few liberties."

"Liberties?" I stared at him in confusion. "What are you talking about?"

"Well…maybe it's better to *show* you than tell you." The smirk on his face said it all: he was getting a kick out of this. He reached for a mirror from the side table next to my bed and handed it to me.

It was then that I saw myself for the first time. And as impossible as I had thought just moments before that I'd ever be able to laugh again when Jackson was around, I erupted into a burst of giggles.

Staring back at me through the reflection was me, but with one, big difference: my hair looked like a hot mess.

"What happened? Why do I look like I have a bird's nest on my head?" The sad attempt of two pigtails down my shoulders wasn't hard to miss. It looked like someone had braided my hair with their eyes closed, and with just one hand. Instead of two braids falling down each side in two straight lines, the braids were crooked with lumps and loose strands protruding from them. What added to the mess were all the knots and tangles in the hair—it looked like my hair had been only partially brushed before it was braided.

"Hmm, really? A bird's nest?" He twisted his face into a serious frown and studied my hair as if he couldn't see the issue. "But I was going for more of a homeless person look."

Then—like second nature—I lifted my hand up and smacked Jackson in the arm. "You're such an asshole."

"Ouch!" He cried out and rubbed his hand up and down his arm. "Sheesh, looks like some things never change."

"This isn't funny," I pouted as I tried to brush out some of the mess with my fingers.

"Well actually, I think it's pretty damn funny." He chuckled and playfully reached for the end of one of the braids.

I swatted at his outstretched hand and made a face at him. "You would."

He laughed. "You would think it's funny too if the situation were reversed."

"I can't believe you," I moaned as my fingers pulled against a large knot of hair.

"Oh come on, Clo. You know if you were me and I had long hair like yours, you wouldn't be able to resist either."

I rolled my eyes. "Jerk." I glared at him, but his smile only grew wider as he watched me with amusement.

"Long live Pippi Longstocking," he responded with glee. Then he scooted onto the edge of the bed, leaned his face next to mine and looked into the mirror that I still held up in front of me.

I watched him studying my reflection from the corner of my eyes and couldn't read the meaning behind the small smile on his face. There were a few moments of silence between us as he continued to look at the mirror and I wondered what he was thinking.

"You know, Pippi," he said thoughtfully and with a straight face. "I really think your hairstyle's making a comeback." Then he exploded into laughter as the warmth of his body pressed against mine.

"Ha ha," I replied sarcastically. "Not funny." I tried to push him off the bed. "You're so mean. You always find so much pleasure in making fun of me."

"Oh come on, Clo." He wrapped his arm around my shoulder and pulled me closer to him. "Don't be mad at me. I'm just playing with you." He looked down at me and grinned. "You know no matter how, umm, *unique* you or your hair looks, I'll still think you're the cutest thing I've ever laid eyes on."

As he beamed down at me with that smile that caused my insides to melt, my body stiffened. Like a cruel joke fate was playing on us, images of the letters in the attic flashed through my mind at that moment, and I was instantly brought back down to reality.

I can't do this. This is wrong. I can't sit here and smile with him, laugh with him, and hit him flirtatiously and pretend to be upset like before.

"What's wrong, Clo?" His face fell when he noticed my changed expression. "Are you okay?"

I drew in a steady breath and forced myself to smile over at him. "Yeah. Nothing's wrong." But I quickly looked away when our eyes met because it was more than I thought I could handle. "I'm…"

Just then, a woman in a white coat knocked on the open door.

I looked over at her eagerly, relieved by the interruption.

"Ms. Sinclair, I'm Doctor Morgan. It's great to see you awake. You really had everyone worried for the last two days. How are you feeling?"

"Hi." I gave her a small smile. "I'm feeling okay. Has it really been two days?" I didn't realize I'd been unconscious for that long.

"Yeah. You were very lucky though. Other than some minor flesh wounds from the car's impact with the water, you didn't sustain any injuries. And thanks to this young man, you were pulled out of the water pretty quickly, so it doesn't look like there was any permanent damage from oxygen deprivation."

I nodded. I knew I should feel lucky and thankful that I was okay. But with Jackson's arm still over my shoulder, that wasn't how I felt—that was the last thing I felt.

"Doctor Morgan, does this mean she can go home soon?" Jackson asked.

"I want to check her vitals and run a few tests, and if everything looks good, she can be discharged as early as tomorrow morning."

"That's great news." Jackson smiled over at me and I saw the relief on his face.

Within a few minutes, Doctor Morgan had checked my vitals and left my room, leaving me alone with Jackson again.

"Alone at last," Jackson said in a playful tone as he reached for my hands. "You know what we need to do when we leave here?"

"What?" I moved my hand away just in time to avoid his touch.

He didn't seem to notice my recoil. "We need to go on our first date."

The clear excitement in his voice broke my heart.

There was a moment of silence before he asked, "Is everything okay, Clo?"

"Yeah. Why?"

"You just seem a little quiet." Jackson watched me carefully.

"Sorry." I faked a yawn. "I just suddenly feel really tired." I slid down the bed and pulled the blanket over my chest.

"Oh okay." He sounded disappointed. "I hope I didn't upset you earlier with your hair. I was just so happy that you woke up that I think I just got carried away with my teasing."

"You didn't upset me, Jax." I fought back the tears as I felt his eyes glued on me. "I'm just tired."

"Okay. I'll let you rest, Clo. But if you need me, I'll be right here, okay?"

I nodded and turned my face away from him, just before tears started rolling down my face. I knew then that there would be no way for me to be with him without wanting more than I could have. As I closed my eyes and pretended to sleep, the ache in my chest had become unbearable to take.

Will this pain I currently feel ever go away? How can I tell Jackson the truth if it means I would be inflicting this kind of pain on him?

I was just about to drift off to sleep when I heard Aunt Betty's hushed voice from the doorway.

"Is she…?" she question trailed off and I heard the fear in her voice.

"She's just resting," Jackson reassured her.

There was a sigh of relief. "Sorry it took us so long to get here, Jackson. We got stuck in rush hour traffic."

"Did the doctor say anything?" Uncle Tom asked.

"Yeah, she said her vitals are strong and the tests all look good. She wants to keep her here overnight for observations but said we can take her home tomorrow."

"That's such a relief, Jackson," Aunt Betty said.

"Aunt Betty?" I shifted in the bed and turned to face them standing at the doorway.

"Oh, honey." She rushed to my side.

I smiled up at her and Uncle Tom, who was leaning over her shoulder.

"How are you feeling, dear?" She leaned over and gave me a hug. Before she pulled away, she whispered in my ear, "Did you let Jackson braid your hair?"

"I feel okay," I answered, choosing to ignore her question about my hair. "It's so good to see you guys."

"We're so glad you're okay," Uncle Tom said as he hugged me. "I don't know what we would have done if…"

"Don't worry." I flashed them a reassuring smile. "I'm okay now." But as my words echoed in my mind, I wondered if I actually meant it. *Was I really okay?*

Chapter Five

CHLOE

Since I'd gotten back home from the hospital yesterday morning, I'd spent most of my time in my bed, trying to shut the rest of the world out. It felt safe there, free from Jackson, free from facing the truth and the pain.

Jackson had called and texted a few times. I never answered the calls or returned them. I'd texted him back once and simply told him that I was tired and wanted some time to myself. I knew he was worried and didn't want to leave me alone. He'd stopped by a few times to check up on me when I stopped responding to his follow-up text messages. But each time he asked to see me, either Aunt Betty or Uncle Tom would turn him away because I wasn't willing to see him. I told Aunt Betty and Uncle Tom that I was too tired and didn't want to see anyone. To my relief, they accepted my request without asking too many questions.

But I knew they were worried. I knew that there was an expiration date on how long they'd let me go on avoiding everything. And the harder I'd tried to not think about him, the stronger Jackson seemed to consume my mind. I knew I had to face reality, and soon.

It was early afternoon when I finally made up my mind on what I was going to do. I wasn't going to tell anyone about what I'd discovered. I was too ashamed and disgusted with myself to say it aloud—to make it feel more real than it was inside. This was going to be a secret I was going to take to my grave.

I also made up my mind that I was going to face Jackson today. I was going to make him forget about me and move on with his life.

So when Jackson stopped by the house and asked about me, I agreed to see him.

I had been preparing myself for this conversation all morning, rehearsing what I'd say to him and mentally preparing myself for his responses. But as soon as he walked into my room and closed the door behind him, I felt a heavy knot twist in the pit of my stomach. It was then when I realized that there was nothing that could have prepared me for this moment. Because no matter what was about to happen, I knew I was going to hurt him, and there was nothing I could do to avoid that outcome.

"Are you okay, Clo?"

I was sitting on top of my bed when he rushed over and gave me a hug. I didn't hug him back.

"I'm fine, Jax." I looked down at my feet, finding it hard to turn and face him. "I'm sorry I haven't been really responsive lately. I've just been really tired since the accident."

From the corner of my eyes, I saw him open his mouth to say something, but stopped. He watched me intently before sitting down next to me on the bed. "Can you look at me?"

I froze, surprised by the bluntness of his question. "Why?" I ended up blurting out.

"Because…" He drew in a sharp intake of breath. "Because you haven't really looked at me for longer than a minute since your accident." His voice was low and uneven.

Guilty wrenched against my insides, knowing that he was already in pain and I was the cause. Fighting back the tears that threatened to break my composure, I clenched my jaw tightly, dug my nails deep against the side of my thigh, and tried to focus on the pain.

"I'm sorry, Jax," I finally said. "I've just been thinking a lot about us since the accident." I tried to focus on the explanation I had thought up and rehearsed before he'd arrived.

"Thinking about what?" There was uneasiness in his question.

"I just think we should put the past behind us, you know? So much as happened between us, I think it's foolish for us to think we have a future together. We're not the same people we were when we were kids. We've both changed in the last nine years apart. We don't owe each other anything. We shouldn't feel obligated to get married just because we made a silly pact when we were kids."

There was a moment of silence as he took in my words. "You're not making sense, Clo," he said softly. "I don't feel obligated to do anything. That's not how I feel about you or what we have. This has nothing to do with the pact." He grabbed ahold of my hands and squeezed them tightly between his. "This has *everything* to do with how I feel about you. There's something special between us and I've known that for a very long time. I know you have, too. That kiss we shared the other night by the lake? *That* was real."

Unable to respond with words, I shook my head violently.

Suddenly, before I could stop him, he grabbed my face and pulled me toward him. His mouth greeted mine with hunger as his tongue forced my lips apart. For a split second, I kissed him back, unable to control my own desire as my lips and tongue moved with his.

"No! We can't," I cried out as I pushed him away violently when I realized what we were doing. "I can't," I said as I wiped my lips with the back of my hand and gasped for breath.

"Why?" he demanded as he grabbed my arms and started to shake me. "Give me one reason why!"

"Because…" I caught a glimpse of the pain and confusion in his eyes and immediately looked down to the floor. "Because I'm in love with someone else."

He froze as soon as he heard my words. I was riddled with guilt that I had to hurt him with this lie, but I tried to remind myself that I was saving him from the pain of knowing the truth.

"No, you're lying." He took a step back and shook his head in disbelief.

"It's the truth," I tried to convince him. "It's my ex-boyfriend in Los Angeles. He's been trying to get me back and it wasn't until the accident, when I almost died, that I realized that I still want to be with him." I closed my eyes, feeling a wave a shame wash over me, knowing that my lie was hurting the one and only man I loved. *But you can't love him*, a voice reminded me.

Silence fell between us. I could feel his eyes locked on me as I continued to look at the ground. I expected him to accept my lie, give up, and walk away. But I was wrong.

"This doesn't make any sense. At Clara and Sam's wedding last week, you were telling me how much you loved me and asking me to forgive you. And we spent the entire day and night at our spot at the lake. You agreed to go on a date with me. We kissed.

You fell asleep in my arms. I know that meant something to you. I just know it."

"Please don't read into all that, Jax. It'll only hurt you more," I said flatly.

"What are you not telling me, Clo? What exactly happened the other day before the accident? What's changed?"

"I don't know what you're talking about," I managed to say, trying to keep my composure. "Nothing happened. Please just drop it, Jax."

"Damn it, Clo. I've known you since we were seven. I know when something's wrong. Just tell me what it is." His voice grew louder, but he sounded more hurt than angry.

"You don't want to know," I finally said, unable to help myself. I knew he wasn't buying my story.

"You don't know that. I have a right to make that judgment for myself."

"I do know."

"I can deal with it. I don't know what happened or what's wrong, but I know we can face any problem together, Clo. Please let me in and tell me what's going on."

I could hear the turmoil and desperation in his voice, and I felt a crack in my resolve.

"There's nothing you can do, Jax. There's nothing that we can fix or change. I just don't think this will work out. I think we made a mistake in being friends again. Please just accept my decision." I was pleading with him now, willing him to not push me any further before it was too late.

"I don't believe anything you're saying right now. I don't believe this has anything to do with an ex-boyfriend. What are you hiding from me? If you're going to fucking break up with me before you even give us a fighting chance, then at least give me a reason why. You owe me at least that. I won't let this go without knowing why. Please just—"

"I'm your sister, Jax—your *real* half sister, that's why!" The words came out before I could stop it, and as soon as I realized what I'd said, I felt paralyzed with fear.

He fell silent and remained motionless.

When I finally pulled my gaze from the floor and met his gaze, the bewildered look across his face shattered my heart.

Chapter Six

JACKSON

At first, her words made no sense to me, like she was speaking a different language that I'd never heard before. But when my brain finally processed what she had said, her words somehow stayed in the dead-silent space between us, mocking me as I tried to figure out if I had somehow misheard her.

"I'm your sister, Jax—your real half sister."

And just like that, like a flip of a switch, the rug was pulled out from under me and my whole world suddenly changed—shifted and turned upside down in a matter of seconds.

This can't be happening...

When I recovered from the initial shock of her comment, I realized how stupid I was to fall for this joke. This was just her attempt to get back at me for the Pippi Longstocking braids she woke up with at the hospital.

"Don't be ridiculous, Clo. That's not funny at all." I let out a forced laugh. "If you want to get me back for messing with your hair the other day, you should at least say something that's believable."

"I wish it was just a joke, Jax…but it's not. It's very real."

It was then that I finally noticed her clearly. She didn't look like she was joking. She didn't look like she was enjoying this. She looked miserable. There were dark circles underneath her eyes and her face was sunken in like she hadn't slept for days. As she looked at me, I saw the pain in her eyes as her lower lip trembled like she was trying to hold back the tears.

"You're not joking," I muttered, more to myself than to her. I stumbled back a few steps as my legs suddenly gave out on me.

She shook her head solemnly as a few tears rolled down her face.

"But...but how? How can that even be possible?"

She closed her eyes and whispered, "We share the same father."

"Wh—what?" I stammered. "But you and my fa—" I didn't finish my sentence, realizing what I was about to accuse her of.

But she didn't need me to say the rest. She lowered her head and let out a deep, painful sigh. "I didn't know then..."

Suddenly it hit me like a brick. Suddenly I realized why she was pushing me away, why she said we wouldn't work. "And you and me..."

She nodded as drops of tears pummeled to the ground from her face. "We can't...we can't be together."

I shook my head, still unwilling to accept this. "But you still haven't told me why you think we're—I mean, this can't be true. I mean, the two people who would be able to confirm this—your mom and...—they're both dead."

Without a word, I watched her walk over to her desk and pull open the top drawer. She dug through some papers and notebooks before pulling out something from the bottom of the drawer.

Fear shot through my body as I watched her approach me, her eyes seemed to be fixed on a spot on my shirt as she avoided my gaze. Her hand was shaking uncontrollably as she handed me a stack of letters and opened envelopes. From the faded yellow hue of the papers and the worn edges and folds, I knew these letters had been around for a long period of time.

I stared at the stack of letters in her outstretched hand in front me for what seemed like an eternity before I finally reached for them. I didn't want to know what I'd find inside. But this was what Chloe had been hiding from me. She hadn't wanted me to know, but I forced her to tell me. So there was no going back. I had to face whatever I'd find inside these letters.

As soon as I flipped open one of the letters, my chest tightened when I saw—the damning evidence scrawled across the page. "It's his handwriting." The words came out in a low, breathy rush of air. I opened several other letters from the stack, trying to find one that would prove me wrong, trying to find one that would cast some doubt in my mind that these weren't written by him. But each letter I opened was like the last—they all had the same handwriting I knew well. They were all written by my father.

I turned back to the first letter in the stack.

"Judy's my mom," Chloe's tiny voice cut through my daze.

I flipped through the letters again and confirmed what I didn't want to believe. All these letters were addressed to a Judy. I leaned back against the wall and slid to the floor.

Then I started to read through them.

Whatever hope that I had clung onto that this was all a big misunderstanding was slipping from my grasp with each additional letter I read. And then I got to the letter that destroyed any shred of hope I had remaining.

Judy,

You are the world to me, my love. You know that, right? Then you should know how happy I was when you told me that you were pregnant with our child. And only you would be so prepared to be a mother that you've already decided on what you'd want to name your first born. Chloe and Jeffrey are perfect names!

It makes me sad that you were worried at first about telling me. You should know me by now, and you should know that nothing would make me happier than to start a family with you and grow old with you. Don't worry about my parents. They will eventually come around and realize how perfect you are for me. Once I have things figured out with them, I want you to marry me! I hope you say yes, my love.

Always Yours,

John

It was the final nail in the coffin. The smoking gun. I read it again, then again, and then a third time, each time hoping I'd find another explanation that didn't involve my father being Chloe's father.

But I didn't find it.

I looked over at Chloe for the first time since I started reading the letters. She was silent, her eyes wet with sadness.

"I didn't want you to find out," she finally said, her voice barely audible.

"Why?"

"Because I didn't want you to be in this kind of pain."

"So you were going to shoulder the pain for both of us?" I frowned at her and shook my head. "Silly girl," I whispered.

I leaned my head back and pounded my head against the wall. I was defeated and enraged that there was nothing I could do to change things. My hands slumped to my sides, causing the stack of letters to slide off my grasp and into the empty space between us.

"But you're right, Clo." I closed my eyes and let out a heavy sigh. "I can't deal with this reality."

Chapter Seven

JACKSON

"Keep 'em comin', Joe," I said, waving the bartender over to refill my empty shot glass.

"Are you sure, man?" He came over with the bottle of Jim Beam bourbon whiskey. "I just opened this fifth tonight when I opened the bar, and you're the only person who's been drinking it.

I looked at the near half-empty bottle of bourbon in his hands and snorted. "It still looks pretty fucking full to me." I lifted my empty shot glass up at him and motioned for him to pour me another shot.

"If you say so," he said with a shrug and filled my glass to the brim.

I threw back the shot, barely tasting it by this point as it went down as smooth as water.

"Hey, baby," came a woman's voice from behind me.

For a split second, I wondered if it was Chloe. I turned around and frowned. It wasn't her. *Wishful thinking*, I thought.

The blonde who had spoken slid into the stool next to me and flashed me a smile. "You look like you're in need of some company. Wanna buy me a drink?"

My eyes gave her a once-over. She was wearing a tiny red minidress that left very little to the imagination.

"You like what you see?" She bit her bottom lip and leaned into me, letting her full breasts spill over her low-cut top, in perfect line with my vision.

Ignoring her question, I turned back to my empty shot glass and motioned to the bartender for another round.

"I'll have a mojito," the blonde whispered into my ear. Then I felt her wet tongue lick up against my jaw line before she started to nibble my earlobe. At the same time, her hand moved down my side and over my crotch.

My groin tighten in response—aroused and in need of its release. But before the blonde could begin to rub against my growing erection and stimulate it further, I grabbed her hand and pushed her away.

"Nooot interested," I said flatly as I pushed my glass toward Joe as he approached with the bottle of Jim Beam.

"What about my drink?" the blonde pouted, somehow ignoring my brush-off.

I finally turned to her. "What about it?"

"Well aren't you going to order it for me?" She flashed me another smile and flipped her hair over her shoulder.

"Nah." I turned back to my drink and threw it back.

"Why not?" she asked, unwilling to accept my lack of interest.

"Because you're more than capable of ordering and buying your own drink."

"What the fuck is your problem?" She glared at me. "I felt how hard your cock got when I touched it just now. Don't act like you don't want a piece of *this*." She waved her hand down in front of her body.

By this point, the countless shots of bourbon were catching up to me and I was losing my patience.

"Don't flatter yourself. My cock gets hard when I'm drunk. It would get hard even for Joe over there, and I *definitely* don't want to fuck him. So why don't you go whore yourself out to someone who actually wants your STDs and leave me the fuck alone."

Just then, a splash of water hit the side of my face. "Asshole!" the blonde lashed out before storming off.

I knew I was a bit too harsh on the girl, but she was coming on way too strong and didn't seem to get my subtle hints. And tonight, of all nights, was just the wrong night to test my patience. I wiped my face with the back of my hand and motioned for the bartender again. He filled my glass without waiting for me to ask.

I wasted no time and gulped down the liquid. "Leeet me tell ya somethin'," I began to slur as I slammed the empty glass on the counter. "Life's really *fucked* up."

The bartender raised an eyebrow but didn't respond. Instead he humored me and stuck around to listen.

I raised my index finger and waved it in front of me. "You think you finally got it figured out. You think you—you have it all. And when you're just about to be happy with the girl you've wanted for the last twenty-three years, life just shits all over it. Life's a fuuuckin' shitter—a Goddamn shitter."

As the room started to sway around me, I groaned and dropped my head down against the bar to steady myself. "Shit—shitting evvverywhere," I muttered into the   cool, wooden surface.

Then I lifted my head back up suddenly and looked at the bartender. "Does life shit on you, too, Jack?"

"It's Joe," he corrected as he wiped down some of the bourbon that had spilled on the counter.

"Ohh…really?" I shot a doubtful look. Then I bursted into laughter. "That's right. You're Joe. *I'm* Jack." I hit my chest a few times with the palm of my hand to let him know who Jack was. "That's what a lot of people at work call me. Jjjjack." Then I huffed out a heavy sigh. "And then there's one person who calls me Jax. She's the only one that calls me that, and she…" I quickly shook my head in a knee-jerk motion, trying to shake her out of my head. I   lifted my glass up again. "Hit me with another one!"

"Buddy, I think you've had enough."

"Come on, man. Just one more."

Joe sighed and shook his head in pity. "Okay, but after this one, I'm cutting you off and calling you a cab to take you home. I think you've had more than enough for tonight."

I grunted. "Fine. After this one, I'll hit the road, Jack, and I won't-cha come back. No more, no more, no more, nooo morrre." I threw my head back and laughed.

He just stared at me and continued to shake his head.

"Get it?" I looked at him expectantly, "Like that Ray Charles song—oh except…that's riiiight, your name's not Jack." I drained the glass Joe just refilled. "Daaaamn, I keep forgetting." I laid my head back down on the counter and hummed the Ray Charles song to myself.

"Alright, Jack," came Joe's voice a few minutes later. "Your cab's on its way. You need help getting in the cab?"

I threw two hundred-dollar bills on the counter and waved his offer off with my hand. "No thanks, man. I'm really not that drunk," I said just as I got up from the barstool and stumbled over an empty chair nearby. "I had a lot of fun tonight."

"Drink some water when you get in, Jack. You'll thank me for it in the morning."

❦ ❦ ❦

When the cab dropped me off in front of my house fifteen minutes later, I wasn't ready to go to bed. I needed to see her. I needed to talk to her.

So I stumbled over to her house and pulled out my phone to call her.

She didn't pick up.

I went over to the side of the house and looked up into her bedroom window. The lights were off.

I dialed her number again. "Pick up, Clo," I muttered.

Finally, after five or six rings, I heard a click.

"Hello?" came Chloe's half-asleep voice from the other end. "Jax?"

"Heyyy, Clo. What you doing? You busy?" I watched as her window seemed to sway back and forth in front of me.

I heard her moan. "Jax, it's almost two in the morning. What's going on? Why are you calling?"

"I'm downstairs and wanted to see you, that's all. Can you come down and see me?"

"Are you drunk? You sound drunk." I heard the hesitation in her voice.

"Psstt. Nnnoo. Course not." I let out a sigh. "Silly question. Silly girl."

"Jax, I know you're drunk. You need to go home and sleep it off."

"Come on, Clo. Just for a minute. I wanna tell you something."

"What is it?"

"Can you come downstairs?"

"Can this wait until the morning?"

"Pleeeease?"

She let out an exaggerated sigh. "Fine. I'll be right down."

"Cool. I'll be here waiting."

I rushed to the front of the house and waited anxiously for her to come out. A minute later, I heard the sound of the locks on the front door right before she opened it and walked outside.

I smiled the moment I saw her. She looked sexy under the moonlight wearing nothing but grey French terry shorts and a plain white t-shirt. As she walked closer to me, my eyes caught the sight of her hard nipples poking against the thin fabric of her shirt and I felt my erection swell against my jeans.

As if she noticed where my eyes were looking, she folded her arms together as she approached me closer.

"Are you okay, Jax? It's a chilly out. What is so important that you woke me up in the middle of the night to tell me?"

She avoided my gaze and I could tell she was still trying to distance herself from me.

"You want the truth?"

There was a moment of hesitation before she answered. "I'm not sure."

"I miss you, Clo," I blurted out. "I can't stop thinking about you, and it's killing me."

She glanced up at me, and for a brief moment, I saw the anguish on her face. But as quickly as it'd appeared, it was gone. "It's been less than twelve hours since we last saw each other," she said matter-of-factly. "That's not enough time to miss a person."

"Don't be like that. You know what I mean." I took a step toward her.

"No, I don't." She took a step back.

"I just can't do it, Clo. You're right. It's been less than twelve hours, and I already miss you."

"Jax…I think we need some time apart. Maybe…maybe after some time to move past this, we can start spending time together again—as friends, as siblings."

I shook my head, unwilling to ever accept that as a reality. A wave of raw, pent-up emotion, fueled by my intoxication, started to bubble up to the surface.

"I just got you back, Clo," I said in insurgence.

She fell silent and just looked over at me.

"Life is hard as it is, Clo. But it's harder without you there by my side. I have secretly loved you since you were seven and I was eight. I never told you how I felt because I thought you didn't feel the same way, because I didn't want to lose you. But then, when we were in college, when we stopped talking, I thought I lost you then. That was when I started to regret not ever telling you how I felt about you before it became too late. And then after nine years apart, I was given a second chance. I finally had you back in my life, and we had a chance to be together. But just three days ago, when I saw you flying off that bridge in your car, I thought that this time, I had lost you forever. And do you know what?" I paused, feeling the rush of alcoholic adrenaline coursing through my veins, urging me on. "Both times I thought I'd lost you, life felt darker, dimmer, and incomplete because you weren't in my life."

Under the streams of moonlight, she blinked quickly, and I thought I saw a glisten of moisture on her cheek.

Feeling emboldened by liquid courage, I continued in a state of near-madness. "But now that you're okay—now that I just got you back again…I—I just can't—no! I *won't* allow myself to lose you again, Clo! I'll do anything to have you in my life."

Before I knew what I was doing—being driven by a drunken frenzy—I grabbed her and pulled her urgently into my arms.

She cried out in surprise.

"I just can't lose you again, Clo." I held her tightly in my embrace, unwilling to let her go. I buried my face into her hair and drew in a deep breath, intoxicating myself with her scent. As I pressed her against my chest, I felt the hardness of her nipples rub up against my stomach, fueling a need in the pit of my stomach.

"Jax, stop this!" She finally managed to break away and she took several steps back. Her eyes were filled with tears as she shook her head. "You're drunk, Jax. You're belligerent right now. You know we can't do this."

My chest tightened with pain. "But—but I don't want to live a life without you."

She bowed her head and wiped the tears from her face. "You have to," she said in a whisper. "I have to...*We* have to."

"No we don't!" I disagreed. "No one knows about this, and no one has to! Does it really matter who we are? What if we never found out? I love you, Clo. I think about you more than anyone should for a sibling. How can the way I feel be wrong if it makes me happy—if it makes you happy? How can loving the one person that means everything in my life—the one person I've loved since I was eight years old be wrong? You tell me that!" I pointed my finger at her, demanding that she give me a reason I could accept. I knew she couldn't. I knew she loved me too.

"We would know, Jax. We would know the truth."

Suddenly, driven by a second wave of drunken impulse, I dove at her, grabbed her face with my hands and kissed her passionately with complete abandon. I needed her to feel how much I loved her, cared for her, and needed her.

Numbed by raw desire, I didn't register her resistance against my grasp. Instead I parted her lips with my tongue and explored her deeply, pressing my mouth savagely against hers. I grabbed the small of her back with one hand and pulled her body tighter against mine—against my ever-growing erection inside my jeans. I let out a primal groan when her body rubbed against my hardness.

"No! We can't!" she screamed out.

Suddenly, I stumbled backwards. It took me a second to realize that she had pushed me away. I looked over at her, expecting her to be mad at me. But it wasn't anger I saw on her face. It was pain.

"Don't you want us to be happy?" My question came out in a low, defeated voice.

"We can't. We just can't, Jax. This is *not* okay. No matter how much we want it to be okay, we have to accept that it's not okay—it can never be okay."

Then, without another word, she turned and ran back into her house. When I watched her close the door behind her and heard her secure the deadbolt in place, I felt a heaviness in the pit of my stomach.

Could this be it? Could this be how our story ends? Have I lost her for good?

❧❧❧

My head was pounding when I woke up. A constant ringing in my ear only made the headache worse. I smacked the alarm clock on my bedside table to turn it off. But the ringing didn't stop. It was then that I realized the ringing was coming from my phone.

It took every effort to open my eyes against the bright late-morning sun that lit up the room, and when I finally did, I tried to find the source of the noise.

I saw my phone on the floor at the foot of the bed. I reached for it and saw that it was my mother's name on the caller ID.

"Hello?" I croaked into the phone.

"Jackson? Oh thank God, you finally picked up," my mother's distressed voice came through the other end.

"What's wrong, mom?" Something in her voice caused me to sit up from the bed.

"What do you remember from last night?"

"What do you mean?" I tried to think to last night and images of what had happened between me and Chloe outside of her house came rushing back. I groaned, feeling shame for forcing myself on her and feeling sick for the line I made us cross.

"What do you remember?" she asked again.

"Why are you asking me this?" I asked, avoiding her question. "Why do you think anything happened last night?"

"So you don't remember then," she said in an ominous voice.

"Wait, what happened, mom? What's wrong?"

There was heavy sigh. "You were really upset last night, Jackson."

How does she know that?

"You were really drunk and you came home and set off the security alarm system."

"I did?" This was news to me and I walked out of my room and looked down the stairs to make sure the front door was closed. It was.

"Yeah, you did. The alarm company called me at three in the morning, asking me if I was at the house because the alarm was set off. I told them that my son was currently staying there temporarily and told them I'd call you first before having them call the authorities."

"You called me? Did I pick up?"

"Yes, you picked up."

"Oh." I frowned, wondering how long I'd blacked out for last night.

"You started screaming at me when you picked up."

"I did? I'm sorry, mom. I shouldn't have done that. I don't remember any of this. It's not an excuse, but I just had a really bad day yesterday and—"

"Jackson," she cut me off, and from the tone in her voice, I immediately fell silent.

"What is it, mom?"

"We need to talk." She paused and then let out a tired sigh. "There are some things I think you should see. I didn't think they were important to tell you before, but it seems like that's changed. Can you come by my condo today? The sooner the better."

Chapter Eight

CHLOE

I didn't usually wake up early, but this morning, my eyes opened before the sun peaked through my windows. The heaviness I felt when I walked away from Jackson and closed the door between us—and our relationship—stayed with me, and as soon as my eyes opened this morning, it was there, reminding me of what I'd lost.

My thoughts went back to last night and the pain in Jackson's eyes was forever etched into my memory. I hated myself for all that'd happened—for finding those letters, for hurting him time and time again, for not giving in to him last night when he poured out his heart to me.

Last night was the first time he'd ever told me he loved me. They were the words I'd been dying to hear from him. They were the words I'd daydreamed about. They were the words that I'd thought would make me the happiest person on Earth.

But they came too late. When he'd said those words last night, I'd wished he didn't say them. I'd wished he didn't feel that way. Those words only further broke my heart.

I hated myself for hurting him. I hated myself for being cold and distant against his emotional declaration of love. But as much as I had felt the same things he had said, I forced myself to stay strong against his desperate pleas. I knew I couldn't let us cross this forbidden line anymore. I was a sinner. I'd done far too many unforgivable things in my life—some of them, I chose knowingly, some I hadn't.

But Jackson was innocent in all this. I wouldn't be able to live with myself if I dragged him down with me.

I tried to closed my eyes, forcing myself back to sleep so I could escape this reality. But it was useless. I finally rolled out of bed sometime later and jumped into the shower.

By the time I got downstairs, Aunt Betty and Uncle Tom were already downstairs in the kitchen.

"Good morning, honey," Aunt Betty looked up from the eggs cooking on the stove. "I'm making omelets. What would you like in yours?"

I forced a small smile. "Thanks, but I'm not really hungry. I'll just have some coffee."

"You sure, honey?" She eyed me with a concerned look. "You just got out of the hospital. You should get some more nutrients in you. At least have a few bites."

"Okay, sure," I said out of guilt. The last thing I wanted was to make them more worried about me than they were already. "Just scrambled eggs are fine then."

After I forced down a few bites of food during breakfast, I spent the rest of the morning on the couch with Uncle Tom as he watched the marathon of Shark Week on the Discovery channel. Before college, I used to look forward to this week during the summer when Uncle Tom and I would be glued to the television. But it didn't feel the same—my heart wasn't in it. My heart was in mourning.

At some point, I had fallen asleep on the couch because I was woken up by Aunt Betty's hand shaking my shoulder as she called my name.

"Chloe, Jackson's here to see you."

The second his name was mentioned, I bolted upright and was wide awake. "He's here?"

"Yeah, he's at the front door. Do you want me to invite him in?"

"No," I said quickly. "I don't want to see him." I looked over at Aunt Betty with pleading eyes. "Do you mind telling him to leave?"

"Are you sure?" She frowned.

"Yeah. I'm not feeling well right now."

"Okay, I'll let him know."

A minute later, she was back. "Chloe, he says he has something to give you. He said he can leave, if you want him to, after he gives it to you."

My chest tightened with pain and I wondered what Jackson was trying to do this time. I wasn't sure I was ready to face him again. Last night was hard enough as it was to resist him, to hurt him like that. I wasn't sure I could do it again. I wasn't sure I had the willpower to resist my own temptations.

"Can he just leave the item he wants to give me with you? I can contact him later about it."

"I asked him that. He said he has to give it to you in person. He says you'll want to see it and that it'll change everything."

I looked up at Aunt Betty, wondering what Jackson meant by "it'll change everything." "Did you see what he was holding?"

"Hmm. I wasn't really looking, but it looked like a stack of letters or papers."

"Oh." I felt a strong urge to go see what he wanted to show me, but the image of his pained expression from last night stopped me. *Can I do that to him again?*

"Honey, are you guys okay? Did you two have a fight or something?"

"No…It's complicated," I muttered.

"Chloe, I really don't want to interfere with you two, but I know you both care about each other. I'm sure if you guys sat down and talked about it, you can work everything out."

"I don't think that's the case this time."

She sighed. "Honey, just go talk to him. When you were in the hospital, he never left your side for longer than a few minutes. I'm not sure I saw that boy eat or sleep once when I was there. I think you owe it to him to at least give him a few minutes to give you what he has for you and say what he has to say."

Tears welled up in my eyes, wishing things would be different. At that moment, I wished Aunt Betty and Uncle Tom were my parents instead of my aunt and uncle.

"Come on, Chloe. Just give him a minute of your time. If you need me to shoo him away after a minute, I will."

"Does he look like he's been drinking?"

Aunt Betty was taken aback by my question. "No, not that I can tell. He actually looks really excited, almost happy."

"Happy?" I glanced up at her, wondering if I heard her correctly.

"Yeah. He looked anxious but excited and happy about something."

After a few seconds of silence, my curiosity got the best of me and I finally got up from the couch. "Okay, I'll give him one minute."

"Okay, honey. I'll be right here if you need me."

As I walked to the front door, I tried to convince myself that I would be okay after seeing him, that maybe this was the closure we both needed, that maybe because he was sober, he wouldn't lose control like he had last night. Maybe we could actually talk through this and somehow come out of this as friends again.

I took a deep breath to steady myself before I opened the door.

"Clo!" His eyes lit up as soon as he saw me and he pulled me into his arms.

"Jax, stop this," I cried out as I pushed him away. "I thought I made myself very clear last night."

"Clo, it was all a big misunderstanding. I'm sorry about hugging you but I just got so excited to see you and hold you in my arms."

I frowned, confused by his words. "I know you were drunk last night, but I wouldn't call that a misunderstanding, Jax. I know my words upset you, but we need to be adults here. We need to think about what we're doing. You can't just hold me in your arms because you're excited to see me—you just can't. It can't—"

"Stop, Clo," he cut me off from my tirade. "That's not what I mean. The misunderstanding I'm talking about is over the letters you found, about who your father is."

"Shh," I hissed as I quickly rushed outside and closed the front door behind me. "I haven't told Aunt Betty and Uncle Tom yet."

"You won't have to," he said excitedly, almost close to laughter. "You're not my sister, Clo! My dad's not your dad."

I froze and stared at him in disbelief. "What did you just say?"

He grabbed my arms and beamed at me. "You're not my sister. We can be together!" He pulled me into his chest and pulled me tight between his arms. "I'm never going to let you go this time, Clo. Never."

I felt numb with shock, unable to accept his words, unable to allow myself to have any hope that we could be together—that what he was saying was real.

When he finally released me from his embrace, he pulled out a small stack of letters from his back trouser pocket and handed them to me.

I took the stack of letters cautiously. As soon as I saw the handwriting on the first letter, I knew they were John's handwriting.

"Are these the letters I found?" I asked in confusion. I didn't remember Jackson taking the letters with him when I gave them to him to read.

"No, these are different ones. These are new letters my dad wrote to your mom."

"Newer?" I stared at him, unable to process what this all meant.

"Yes, read them." He smiled at me encouragingly, and I couldn't resist wanting to feel as happy as he looked at that moment.

I took a deep breath and sat down on the steps in front of the door. Jackson sat down next to me and watched me anxiously as I started to read the letters.

There were no dates on any of the letters, and the first few I read through were filled with John's regrets and undying love for my mother. He wrote about how much he missed my mother, about how he made a mistake in marrying Jackson's mother, about how he let his family influence his decision and married for the money and prestige Jackson's mother's family would be able to provide him.

But it wasn't until one of the last letters that my name came up, and I heard myself gasp when I read through it.

Dear Judy,

You have no idea how much I've missed you over the years. I know it's been almost twenty years since I've written to you. I guess I was afraid to. During the time I abandoned you and married another, I had written several letters to you. But I was a fool and a coward and never sent those letters to you. I guess I didn't want to admit to you that I was wrong, that I didn't leave you because I didn't love you anymore. I was ashamed for you to know that I was selfish and picked money and power over our love. And now that I'm writing this letter years later, I know I couldn't send this letter to you even if I wanted to because you're already gone.

I know I've wronged you in so many ways and I'm filled with regret that I was never able to make it up to you. Before you passed away, I hurt you by leaving you at your time of need and marrying someone I didn't love to make my parents happy. And even after you've passed away, I seem to continue to hurt you with what happened with Chloe.

She's beautiful, and I watched her grow up knowing that she was your daughter. The older she got, the more she resembled you. And the more she resembled you, the more I missed you. I missed you so much—your smile, your caress, your love.

When Chloe grew into her body and became an adult, I found myself drawn to her, and sometimes I'd imagine that she was you in the room with me. By the time she started college, she looked exactly like you when we were together and in love.

Judy, I'm a weak, broken man. I'm not a good man. I did something unforgivable, something I hate myself for, something I know you'll hate me for. My desperate longing for you manifested into my desire to have Chloe at any cost. I broke up the love and bond your daughter had with my son so I could have her for myself. I cornered your daughter and slept with her against her will. I missed you so much that I thought that if I had her, I could feel just a small fragment of our love again. But I didn't, and yet I continued trying for over a year before she ended it.

I hate myself for being this sick, perverted man, Judy. I know I am no longer the man you fell in love with. So I know I'm asking a lot, but can you ever forgive me for what I did? I just missed you so much over the years. I was devastated when you had the miscarriage and we lost our unborn child. And instead of being there for you, my grief consumed me and I left you for a loveless marriage. I left you when you needed me the most. I know because of me, you started drinking. I know I ruined your life.

And now, as I am lying here on my deathbed, waiting for the cancer to kill me, I'm completely alone and filled with so much regret. Of all my regrets, my biggest one is leaving you thirty-three years ago when I still loved you. I still love you. I will continue to love you until my very last breath.

Please forgive me.

Always Yours,

John

I stared out into the front yard for what seemed like forever as I tried to process what I'd just read.

It was Jackson who broke the silence. "I talked to my mom this morning and she gave me these letters."

"She had them?" I asked softly, trying to piece everything together in my head.

"Yeah. Even though my parents were divorced by the time my dad passed away from prostate cancer last year, he had left everything to my mom in the will, including the house. After he passed, my mom went and cleaned out the house and found these unsent love letters."

"Did she know about my mom?"

"She said looking back, she knew something wasn't right when she married my dad. They got married pretty quickly after they started dating, because my mom got pregnant with me a few months after they started dating. She said she had seen your mom next door sometimes and thought she saw glimpses of my dad looking out toward your house. But back then, she didn't want to believe there was anything wrong, so she turned a blind eye from those suspicions."

"Oh."

"So you see, Clo. We're not brother and sister. We *can* be together." He grabbed my hands with his and squeezed them.

I met his warm gaze and saw how relieved and happy he looked. But for some reason, I didn't feel that way.

"What's wrong, Clo?" he asked, detecting my mood.

"I guess it's just a lot to take in right now." I sighed.

"But aren't you happy we can now be together?"

"Jax," I began. I couldn't believe I was going to say this after finding out the truth. "I need some time to think."

"Time?" His face fell. "How much time?"

"I don't know," I said honestly.

"A couple of hours? A few days? A week? Ballpark," he urged, somewhat impatiently.

"I don't know, Jax." I got up from the concrete steps and headed to the front door. "I just need some time to process everything."

Without another word, I went inside and closed the door behind me.

"Chloe?" Aunt Betty's head popped out from the kitchen. Then she saw my expression and immediately rushed over. "What's wrong? What happened?"

She sat me down at the dining table and listened to me retell everything that'd happened in the last few days. It wasn't until I finally finished telling her about the new letters I just read that she finally spoke.

"Honey, I know your mom's had a hard life," she said softly. She let out a heavy sigh before continuing, "And sometimes I do blame it on the way John had treated her."

"You knew about them?" I looked at her in surprise.

She nodded. "Your mom met John when she was visiting here one summer. She was a free-spirit then. She was young and didn't have a job, so she lived with us for some time. John lived next door. The house used to be his parents' before they moved down to Florida for warmer weather. They had a short but intense love affair, and from what your mom told me, his family didn't approve of her. John's from a conservative family with a lot of old money and there was an expectation to find a wife with the right pedigree."

"Pedigree?"

"Yeah, like an Ivy League education and an established family name."

"Oh."

"But then your mom got pregnant. At first she told me he was going to tell his parents and marry her, but after she had the miscarriage, things seemed to change. He stopped seeing her and taking her calls. And about six months later, we saw in the papers that he was engaged to the woman who's a part of the Astor family, a rich and influential family since the 19th century."

"And that's Jackson's mom?"

She nodded.

"So who is my father then?" I was afraid to ask but I knew there was no turning back at this point.

Aunt Betty let out a deep sigh. "Your mom was in a bad place after the miscarriage. She started drinking and doing drugs to escape. I think at some point, she found out that Jackson's mom was pregnant, and she wasn't able to cope with that news. Days, sometimes weeks, would go by when she would just disappear because she was out drinking, doing drugs and sleeping around. I tried to reason with her and tried to get her help, but she wouldn't let me. It only made her disappear for longer periods of time. And then one day, she came home sober and told me she was pregnant and needed my help to stay clean because she was determined to keep the baby."

She paused and looked at me. Tears blinded my eyes as I knew what she was going to say next.

"That baby was you, Chloe. When your mom found out she was pregnant with you, she didn't touch a drop of alcohol or drugs. That's how much she wanted you."

Tears streamed down my face as I thought about what my mother had gone through, what she had felt when the man who she loved abandoned her the way he had.

"I miss her," I said as I wiped away my tears.

"Me too, honey. She loved you very much."

There was a long stretch of time where neither one of us spoke. Finally, it was Aunt Betty who broke the silence.

"I'm glad you know the truth now. We almost lost you a few days ago because you didn't know it."

I nodded.

"And now you and Jackson can work through this and start that relationship you've both been denying yourselves for so many years."

"Really? Even with what happened between my mom and his dad?"

"Oh, honey. That was a long time ago. Learn from your mom's mistakes and let go of the past. You are not your mom and Jackson is not his dad. Don't let their mistakes come between what you and Jackson have. You two are perfect together and I know you love each other. Both of you deserve to be happy."

"Yeah." As much as I knew Aunt Betty was right, I couldn't help but feel guilty for wanting to be happy with Jackson.

Aunt Betty left me to myself for the rest of the afternoon when I told her I wanted some time to think. I spent the time lying on my bed, trying to figure out what to do.

I'd held on to the idea of a future with Jackson for so many years that it didn't even feel real anymore. *Did we really love each other? We haven't been friends for almost a decade. So many things have happened between us since then. We may miss our childhood friendship, we may love who we used to be when we were younger, but how do we know we really love each other now? Do we need more time to be just friends to figure things out?*

"I need a sign," I whispered aloud as I looked up at the glow-in-the-dark stars on my ceiling.

I got up from my bed and decided to do some laundry. That always helped me keep my mind off things. I collected some dirty clothes from the floor, checking all the pockets to make sure I didn't wash anything I shouldn't.

When I checked one of my jeans, I felt a piece of paper in the front pocket. I pulled it out, wondering what it was. I didn't remember putting the paper there.

I gasped when I unfolded the paper and saw that it was a note from Jackson.

Dear Chloe,

Last night seemed like a vivid memory from our childhood, and for the first time in almost a decade, I felt that pure happiness of having you by my side return to me. It was a feeling I'd never thought was possible again. But when I woke up this morning to see you still fast asleep in my arms, I knew what I felt last night had been real, and not a dream. Right now, the sun is just starting to come out over the horizon. It's starting to cast its pale yellow light across your face, and I am in awe with how beautiful and peaceful you look asleep next to me. I'm not sure how I lived without seeing your face for nine years.

As much as I've wanted to resist it, my heart has continued to reach out for you over the years. The hatred I had held onto toward you was built upon the intense hurt and love I'd always had for you. Maybe it'd been fate trying to tell me something, but earlier this week, a quote in the newspaper had caught my eye: "Forgiveness is me giving up my right to hurt you for hurting me." It'd come at the perfect time. It'd been right after that night at the wedding reception, that night you'd poured your heart to me as I sat there ignoring you. And when I went to find you after you ran off in tears, I saw you collapse to the ground and at that moment in time, I thought I might have lost you.

It was then that I'd realized that forgiveness may be the ultimate display of love. And if I truly loved you like I'd always thought I had, then forgiveness was something I had to learn to do.

Please give me time to forgive you, and please also try to forgive me for all the times I'd hurt you, forsaken you, and disappointed you. Despite everything that'd happened between us, I am choosing to hold onto the moments that my heart cares for the most: the moments I'd fallen in love with you again and again.

Here's to many more of those moments.

Love,

Jackson

Fresh tears stung my eyes and I reread the letter.

"What am I waiting for?" This was the sign I needed, the sign I'd asked for. "I'm also going to choose to hold onto to the moments that my heart cares for the most, Jax."

I quickly ran out of my room and down the stairs.

"I'm going to go see Jax, Aunt Betty. Be back later," I said as I swung open the front door and headed out toward Jackson's house.

Chapter Nine

CHLOE

There was a surprised expression on his face when he opened the door and saw me smiling up at him.

"I think I just needed a few hours to think things through," I explained.

"Really? So does this mean…? Are we…?"

I giggled. I could tell he was suddenly nervous, which sent a jolt of anxious excitement to wash over me.

"Shit. I haven't felt so tongue-tied in my life." He ran a hand through his dark brown hair, tossing it out of place. I resisted the urge to lean over and smooth his hair.

"Why are you tongue-tied though? It's just me."

"Do you really not know, Clo?" He looked at me expectantly as if he was waiting for me to laugh and admit I was pulling his leg.

I shook my head, unsure of what he was getting at. "What am I supposed to know?"

"Clo, it's not *just* you. It *is* you. I'm tongue tied because I'm nervous. This moment has been a long time coming for me, and I don't want to fuck it up again. I've loved you since I first saw you."

"Oh." I felt lost for words. Hearing him say he loved me at that moment was different than when he said it last night. It felt more real. Suddenly I became nervous, too. This was my best friend, but he was also a man—a very handsome, desirable man who managed to make my heart flutter with just a look and a smile.

"I guess I am trying to ask you out, but when I'd imagined this conversation happening in my head all day today, I'd thought I would be suave and charming, and you would fall head over heels in love with me before we even went on our first date."

"I think you've accomplished that," I said as I met his intense gaze. They were like pools of warm liquid, and I felt myself drowning in their bottomless depth.

He pulled me into his arms and said in a low, deep voice, "Chloe Sinclair, are you ready to be my girlfriend?"

I beamed at him. As he looked into my eyes, I just knew. Those familiar warm, green eyes that I'd longed for in the nine years we'd been apart, the same ones that made me feel at home. There were no more questions or doubt in my mind. We'd been heading this direction since we were seven.

"I've never been more ready."

Our lips met in a long, tender kiss that took my breath away. The rest of the world disappeared around us as we lost ourselves in each others' arms, finally making up for all the years we'd lost.

Chapter Ten

CHLOE

I stepped out of Penn Station in New York City with a huge smile on my face. Jackson had to head back to work in New York City this past Monday. We'd been officially dating for the last two weeks, four days, and three hours—not that I'd been counting—and even though we'd only been apart for the past four days, I was surprised by how much I'd missed him.

Just then, as if he knew I was thinking about him, my phone was ringing with his number on the screen.

"Hey you!" I said excitedly as I stood in the designated line to wait for a cab.

"Hi, babe. I can't wait to see you tonight. When are you leaving for the train station?"

"Mmm, probably not for another hour or so." I grinned to myself as I looked around. I felt sneaky that I was already in New York City without telling Jackson. But I had a little surprise for him.

"What's all that noise in the background? Are you outside?"

"Ohh, I'm just walking around Philly, doing some window shopping," I lied. *Crap*, I thought and tried to cover my phone from some of the noise from the hustle and bustle of the city.

"That sounds like fun."

"So what are you up to right now?" I asked, trying to figure out where he was.

"I'm at the office getting some work done before you get in tonight."

"Are you guys busy today?"

"Nah. Just some paperwork. It's Friday and it's the summer, so half the office is gone because of Summer Fridays."

"Summer Fridays?"

"Oh yeah, it's when people only work a half day on Fridays during the summer. A lot of companies in New York and the area honor it because it gives people time to get to the beaches for the weekend.

"Sounds like fun. How come you're working the whole day then?"

"Well, I did just take two weeks off work when I was back home, so I wanted to use the extra time to get some work done."

"Oh ok. But you're not busy right now, right?"

"No, just paperwork. So don't worry, I'll be all yours tonight."

I giggled. "You better be. Well, I should get going. I'll see you tonight?"

"I can't wait to see you, babe."

I smiled as I got off the phone. "You'll get to see me a little sooner than you think, Jax," I said to myself.

When I got in my cab, I told the driver the address to Jackson's office.

Twenty minutes later, I was taking the elevator up to Jackson's office.

"Excuse me, are you Chloe?" asked the man who was also in the elevator.

I looked over at and didn't recognize him. "Yeah, I am. Have we met?"

He laughed. "No, not yet. I'm one of Jackson's colleagues. Nick Santos. Jackson's been talking about you nonstop at the office and he showed me a picture of you the other day. So I thought you looked familiar."

"Oh, you're Nick. Jackson's mentioned you before too."

"Jackson didn't tell me you were coming into the office today."

"Oh yeah. I'm surprising him." I looked at him sheepishly. "Can you keep it a secret?"

He laughed. "Well I'm sure he's about to find out soon."

I giggled and nodded.

"You know, I've never seen him like this before. He's never been this happy with any other girl he's dated since I've known him."

"Really?" I smiled to myself. "Thanks, Nick. Jax talks about you, too. You're one of his closest co-workers here. He said you've helped him a lot."

"Oh is that so?" He looked pleased. "I'm glad he thinks that of me." He leaned in and whispered, "You know your boyfriend is like the company favorite among the VPs here. Harvard grad who's modest amongst his peers but a shark in business deals for his clients—that's hard to find—I've even heard the CEO joke that he's like the Holy Grail associate."

"Yeah, he's amazing." I beamed, feeling a sense of pride for Jackson. Since as long as I'd known him, he was great at everything. But being his best friend, I'd also watched him work his ass off, too. Nick was right. Jackson was always modest in front of others, and those who didn't know him well had no idea how much work he put into everything. All they saw were the results, and Jackson was always the best at everything.

"I can tell you make him really happy," Nick continued as the elevator doors opened to Jackson's floor. "He's a good guy, Chloe. Don't let him go."

"I won't. I know I'm really lucky." I stepped out of the elevator.

"So Jackson's office is to the right, at the end of the hall," Nick explained as we got to a hallway that went both left and right.

"Office 1568, right?"

"I believe so. His name will be next to the number. I'm on the left end of the hallway, so if you have any questions, let me know."

"Thanks, Nick." I smiled at him gratefully and waved goodbye as I made a right into the hallway.

Just before I got to the door to Jackson's office, I smiled. His office door was opened, but I could hear him talking on the phone with a client.

When I heard his call end, I reached for my cellphone and stepped into an empty cubicle and called him.

"Hey, babe," he said when he picked up. "Miss me already?"

I giggled softly. "Yeah, I really do. What are you up to right now?"

"Still in the office doing some paperwork. Why are you whispering?"

"Am I?" I asked, playing coy. "So you know how you said you can't wait to see me when we talked earlier?"

"Yeah."

"Did you mean it?" I asked with a smile on my face.

"Do you even have to ask me that?" he asked with a light laugh. "I'm dying to see you tonight."

"So does that mean there's something else you rather be *doing* than your paperwork?"

I heard a sharp intake of breath on his end and I smiled. He knew exactly what I was suggesting. For the past two weeks since we'd been dating, we acted like innocent teenagers and hadn't made love yet. Jackson had insisted on taking things slow. But being away from him all week, I didn't think I could wait any longer to be with him.

"Don't you think we've waiting long enough, Jax?" I asked when he didn't respond. "I mean, haven't you missed me all week? Don't you want to be doing…me?"

"I think you're right," he said, almost panting. "If you were here, I would show you just how right you are."

"How would you show me?" I whispered seductively.

"You'd have to wait and see," he flirted back.

"I heard you're a pretty hard worker around here. Would you work just as hard when you're doing me?"

His breathing grew heavier over the phone. "No. I'd work even *harder.*"

"Is that a promise?"

"Fuck yeah."

I let out a soft moan so he could hear how excited I was at this promise.

"Fuck, Clo. I wish you were here already. Have you gotten on the Amtrak yet?"

"No, not yet." I stifled a giggle and felt relieved that he didn't know where I was right now. "If I was there already, what would you be doing to me?"

"If you were here right now, baby, I'd grab your hand and make you feel how hard you've made me."

I slowly drew in an uneven inhale of breath and I felt my stomach flip in excitement. I walked quickly to the door of his office. "What would you do next?"

"You're killing me here, Clo," he groaned.

"Want to know something, baby?" I whispered into the phone.

"What?"

"I'm wearing a dress today and I forgot to put on any panties."

I smiled with satisfaction when I heard him inhale sharply.

"And," I continued, "I'm already really wet thinking about how hard you'd feel...not in my hands, but deep inside me."

"My God, Clo." He started panting more heavily. "If you were here, I'd torture you like you're torturing me now. I'd tease you slowly. First with my fingers because they'll want to explore you and make you dripping wetter than you are now. Then, my mouth and my tongue will get jealous, so they'll need to taste every inch of you. But I wouldn't let you come. I'd wait until you're begging me to fuck you before I make passionate love to you."

I let out a low moan and said, "What if I started begging you now?"

"Don't tease me, woman! If you were here now, you wouldn't need to beg because I'd be all over you before you can even say the word, 'beg.'" he grunted in frustration, causing me to smile triumphantly.

I got to the opening of his opened door and saw that he was in his chair facing the window directly across from the door.

"Beeeeg," I said into the room with a slow, seductive voice.

He immediately jumped and whipped around, his eyes surprised and filled with a raw need that I hadn't seen before.

"Baby, I don't think I've needed anyone more than I need you right now." He stood up and I gasped as my eyes grew wide at the sight of his erection through his pants.

I walked inside his office and immediately closed the door behind me. "So does this mean you don't want to take it slow anymore?" I flashed him a coy smile. All of a sudden, I felt nervous and giddy. It was as if I saw him for the very first time. He was tall, handsome, with an olive complexion and rich green eyes.

"We've taken it slow for over twenty-three years," he said as he walked toward me and found my waist. He pulled me into him and kissed me deeply. When he pulled away, he groaned, "We can't take it any slower." The hot breath of his deep, raspy voice tickled the sensitive skin on my neck and I arched my chest toward him in desire.

I felt his strong, callused hands push down the spaghetti straps of my dress, revealing my sheer ivory bra. He slowly slid my dress down my body, lingering inch by inch as he watched me become increasingly impatient under his touch. He then unhooked my bra, and when my breast spilled out into his hands, he inhaled sharply, his eyes blazed with lust as they took in my nakedness.

"You're so fucking hot." He massaged my breasts with both hands and guided them into his mouth, one at a time, savoring them slowly. I gasped as his mouth inhaled me, his tongue eagerly flicking and nibbling on my hard, excited nipples.

"Baby, it's my turn to taste you," I moaned. I grabbed him and pushed him around and up against the frame of the door. I got down on my knees and grabbed his erection with my hand. "Tell me you're ready for me, Jax," I purred as I felt the power of his rock-hard shaft with my grasp.

"Fuck, baby. You're killing me."

I could see the frenzy in his eyes as I gently traced the outline of his cock with my fingertips. I looked up at him and watched his reaction to my every move, relishing in the growing desire that spread across his twisted face. Without warning, I wrapped my lips around him and slowly and eagerly inhaled the entire length of his cock.

His head jerked back in pleasure and he let out a loud, primal roar as my tongue worked its way up and down the back side of his cock in unison with my lips. He watched me move up and down him, his eyes glowed with smoldering pleasure as I moved more rapidly around his erection.

"Clo, you feel amazing," His voice was strained as he convulsed each time my tongue reached the tip of his cock. "I can't hold on much longer and I need to fuck you bad," he groaned hoarsely.

Instead of stopping, I moved up and down the length of his cock faster and deeper as I began to deep throat him.

"Fuck, you're pushing me over the edge soon!"

Then I stopped. "No. I want you to make love to me now and come inside me," I demanded.

Without waiting another second, he pulled me up and lifted my legs up around his waist and carried me to his desk. In one swift movement, he pushed his paperwork off the desk and laid my back on top of his cool, mahogany desk. "You planned to surprise me like this because you knew I wouldn't be able to resist you."

I gave him a devious smile. "Mayyybe..." I giggled. "I've been pleasuring myself all week while I thought about you and missed you. I just couldn't wait any longer."

"Me either, baby. Now it's my turn to pleasure you," he said in a low, hoarse voice.

I writhed under his touch as I felt his hands slowly run up the length of my legs—from my ankles to my knees to my inner thighs, where I felt his thumbs linger at the edge of my opening. Our eyes met, and as he held my gaze, he moved my feet up to the edge of the desk and spread my knees wide before him.

"Fuck, you're so wet," he groaned when he saw my pussy. His. He lowered his face down between my legs. Then he looked up at me and I saw his eyes roll back in pleasure as he inhaled me deeply. Then he spread my knees farther apart, and I gasped as his mouth began to devour me, causing my whole body to quiver in pleasure. He licked and sucked and tasted me, and before long, I arched my convulsing body against his tongue and found my release.

"Wow. That was amazing," I said with a sigh as I pulled him up to kiss me, my lips tasting my juices on his mouth. "I love the way I taste in your mouth."

"I love the way you taste in my mouth, too."

Then he grabbed my hand and pressed it up against his throbbing cock. "So what are we going to do about this?"

"I think you've been tortured long enough." I pulled out a condom and pulled it down onto his cock. I smiled up at him. "Make love to me, Jax. I want to feel every single rock-hard inch of you inside me."

"God, I love you, Clo," he groaned.

I pulled him to me and kissed him again. "I love you, Jax. I've waited a very long time for you to make love to me." I guided him to my entrance and I welcomed the entire length of his cock deep inside me in one slow and hungry thrust. I cried out and tightened my grip around him, causing him to throw his head back in pleasure.

"Clo, you're so tight! You feel so fucking amazing." He grabbed my ass and started pounding into me. Slowly at first, but with every additional thrust, deeper and harder, pushing out uncontrollable gasps and moans from my lips. I gripped his broad, muscular shoulders, digging my nails into his skin as I moved my hips in time with his thrusts.

After several minutes of sheer bliss, my muscles began to clench around him.

"God, I'm about to come again," I gasped as I looked up at him.

"Me too!" he roared as he dove harder into me. His entire body began to convulse, and seconds later, we both reached the brink of ecstasy.

❦❦❦

After my early surprise visit, Jackson decided to take the rest of the afternoon and enjoy his summer Friday. We walked around the bustling streets lined with shops and bars in the Lower East Side, enjoying the warm, afternoon sun and people watching.

When we passed by a vintage jewelry shop called Doyle & Doyle, something at the window caught my eye.

"Wanna go in and take a look?" Jackson asked when he noticed that I saw something.

"No, it's okay." I smiled over at him. It was clear that this jewelry shop had a lot of engagement and wedding rings. I didn't want him to get the wrong impression.

"Are you sure? I've heard of this place before. They carry a lot of vintage high-end jewelry. Some of my female co-workers gush about this place."

"You know me, Jax. I'm not really into jewelry. So we don't have to go in."

"Come on, it'll be fun. My co-workers seem to love coming in here and trying on the different pieces. We can pretend to be engaged or something, so you can try on the different rings."

I took another glance at the beautiful vintage ring that had caught my eye and I felt myself give in to the temptation. I grinned over at him. "Okay, let's pretend."

I tried on almost a dozen different engagement rings. They were all vintage, gorgeous, and expensive. I almost fainted when I saw the price tags on the rings I'd tried on.

"So babe, which one do you like the most," Jackson looked over at me as I looked at all the rings

I'd tried on sitting on the black, velvet tray in front of me.

I picked up the first ring I'd tried on—the one that caught my eye in the window display. "I still love this one the most." I put it back on my finger and smiled at how brilliant and dazzling it looked. *One can dream*, I thought to myself.

"Your fiancé has amazing taste, Mr. Pierce. That's a 3.8 carat Asscher cut engagement ring. It has two Baguette cut diamonds on each side of the center stone. It's a rare vintage piece, made in 1923. You can say it's almost one of a kind. We just got this in yesterday morning and I'm pretty sure this one will be sold by the end of the week. Would you like to—"

"I'd like to sleep on it," I cut in before we're made to feel guilty if we didn't get the ring. "Thanks so much for your time."

As soon as we got out of the shop, I started giggling. "That was fun, Jax."

"It was fun for me, too."

"Really?" I looked over at him with a raised eyebrow. "Should I be concerned that my boyfriend likes jewelry?"

He laughed. "Don't worry. I'm not metrosexual. You know me well enough to know I'm more of a man's man."

"Mmm-hmmm." I flashed him a suggestive smile.

"I just meant I liked watching you try them on. Your eyes just lit up like you're a fat kid in a candy shop."

I laughed. "Whatever. I'm not into jewelry remember? It was just fun to play pretend, that's all."

"Riiight." He sounded unconvinced.

Then he grabbed a hold of my waist and pulled me into him. "I've missed you, Clo."

I looked up at him. "I missed you, too."

"Move in with me, Clo."

"What?" His words caught me by surprise.

"Would you want to move to New York and move in with me? I don't think I can do long-distance with you. It'd drive me crazy."

"Really?" I felt excited about his offer, because I felt the same way, I wasn't sure I could handle long-distance dating. But I also wanted him to be sure.

"Yes, I'm serious, Clo. I know you're in between jobs right now. So why not look in New York City? There are more opportunities here than in Philly."

"Aren't you worried we're moving a little too fast? We've only started dating two weeks ago. Are you sure you'd want me to live with you?"

"Baby," he said as he looked deep into my eyes, "To me, we're not moving fast enough. I've been courting you for over twenty-three years. So say yes that you'll move to New York."

"Yes." I nodded excitedly, unable to contain myself.

As we walked hand-in-hand to his condo in the East Village, I felt so happy that I had to pinch myself to make sure that this wasn't all a dream.

And it wasn't.

Chapter Eleven

JACKSON

"I've really missed hanging out in your room." I had my arms crossed behind my head.

"Are you sure you're not missing Harvard already?" she asked in her teasing tone.

"Nope. I'm pretty happy being right here hanging out with you."

"So you're not missing those Harvard girls...like Amber?" She looked away when she asked her question.

"Come on, Clo. None of those girls—especially Amber—means anything to me. I'm sorry you walked in on that. I know you don't like her, and I don't ever want you to think that I'd ever pick her over you."

She nodded but didn't say anything.

"Clo, I've really missed you this past semester. We barely talked and I was miserable. We only have half the summer left before we have to go back to school. Can we just move on from what happened and hang out like we used to? Please?"

She finally met my gaze and smiled. "You're right, Jax. I don't want to think about our past or what we've done. Let's just enjoy our time together."

"Great," I said with a wide smile. I turned to lie on my stomach and looked over her shoulder. "What are you reading?"

"Just this book I picked up from the book store last weekend. It talks about setting your goals and dreams for life and not wasting the limited time we have on Earth."

"Oh."

"Jax, tell me about your dreams?"

I frowned. "Why do you want to know what I dreamt of last night?"

She stared at me in disbelief. "Did you listen to anything I said about what I was reading?"

I looked away sheepishly. "Sorry, my mind kind of wandered off."

She shook her head and started laughing. "Sometimes, Jax, I really have no idea how you got into Harvard."

"Hey, don't be mean," I objected but laughed along with her. "You know I don't like to read that kind of stuff. I've never been good with the liberal arts stuffs. That's why I'm taking the business and economics courses."

She rolled her eyes.

"So ask me again," I insisted, not wanting to get her upset.

"Ok, fine. What are your dreams for the future?"

I frowned. "I don't have any real dreams. Does getting a good job after college count?"

She shrugged. "Yeah that does. Do you have a goal of when you want to accomplish that?"

"As soon as possible?" I said in the form of a question and laughed. "What about you? What are your dreams, Clo?"

She looked over at me. "You really want to know, or are you just humoring me?"

"I really want to know."

"Well, besides wanting to find a good job after college, my life goals are I really want to find the one I'm going to love and marry by thirty, get married by thirty-two, have my first child at thirty-four, and then maybe a second child a year after that."

"Oh." I hadn't realized she was talking about those types of goals.

"I know they're odd goals when we're only twenty and in college. But I've always wanted that perfect family with two kids, and being happy together. It's something I always wanted for myself growing up."

I put my arm around her to comfort her. "Don't worry, Clo. I know you'll reach your goals. Besides, you always have me as your safety net. Remember our pact?"

She smiled at me. "That's assuming you don't go and marry some floozy before you turn thirty," she teased.

"Hey, why do you automatically think I'll end up with a floozy?"

She laughed. "Your reputation precedes you."

❦ ❦ ❦

My eyes grew wide when I saw her come into the living room, and as I looked her up and down, a hardness grew inside my pants as I inhaled in a ragged breath. She was wearing an emerald green dress that fell just above the knee. The thin fabric clung to her sexy voluptuous body in all the right places.

"Damn, Clo. I'm not sure I can go out tonight with you looking like that."

"Why? What's wrong with it?" She looked worried as she looked at herself in the full-length mirror.

"Nothing. I just meant, I'm not sure I would be able to take my hands off you if you're looking like that. The things I might do to you in public might raise some eyebrows, even by New York City standards."

Her cheeks flushed red. "Does this look appropriate for tonight?" She shifted uncomfortably in the dress, suddenly self-conscious from the attention I was giving her.

"Baby, it's my birthday party. That's more than appropriate for tonight." I licked my lips. "But I'd rather have you to myself. Let's skip tonight and just stay in so I can remove that dress from your body with my teeth and make love to you all night."

"Jax, don't be silly," she dismissed, but I could tell from the smile on her face that she was happy with my comment. "We have to go. I've invited all of your friends and colleagues to it."

"I know, babe. I was just joking. I know you put a lot of effort into planning this birthday party for me."

She walked over and wrapped her arms around my neck as she sat on my lap. "Happy thirty-second birthday, Jackson." She leaned in and kissed me.

I pulled her down and deepened the kiss, pushing my tongue past her lips and exploring her mouth. She let out a sigh as her hands moved through my hair, urging me on. I felt my cock respond to her on my lap and my hips rocked upward against her ass.

Then she pulled away. "No funny business, or we're going to be late, Jax."

"Come on, Clo. Give me ten minutes," I begged.

She shot me a doubtful look. "When have we ever had gone for ten minutes or less?"

I snickered. "Touche."

"I'm hailing us an Uber now. So come on, let's head downstairs."

"You are such a tease, baby."

She flashed me a sexy smile. "Don't worry, Jax. We'll have plenty of hot sex tonight when we get home."

"You promise?"

"Well, if I break my promise, I'll let you spank me later." She winked at me before heading down the hall for her coat.

"Deal! Please break that promise!" I yelled after her.

❦❦❦

"Jax, great party!" Nick exclaimed as he gave me a handshake and a half-hug.

"Thanks, Nick. This was all Clo's hard work." I looked around the lounge and saw Chloe talking to Nick's wife Julie near the bar.

"She's a keeper, man. I think she's great for you."

I smiled as I watched Chloe laughing about something Julie had just said. "I really love her. I'm glad she and Julie are friends now. It can be hard making friends in a new city, so I'm happy to see Julie's introducing her to all her friends   here."

"Yeah, Julie really likes spending time with her." Nick took a sip from his bourbon. "So are you about to pop the question soon?"

I was taken aback by his question.

"No offense man," Nick added quickly and raised his hands up defensively. "Julie was curious and told me to ask. You know how women are."

I looked over at Chloe and Julie again. "Yeah. Well, we've only been dating for about eight months, so I don't know if it's too soon."

Nick nodded. "Yeah I get it, but haven't you guys been friends since you guys were in diapers?"

I laughed. "Something like that."

"But don't wait too long, man. Chloe's a catch and you two really are great together."

"Yeah. Maybe when we hit our one year anniversary, I'll start thinking about it. I'm just enjoying our relationship and being with her. I don't want to rush her into anything."

"Sounds like a plan." He looked at his near-empty glass. "I'm going to grab another drink. Let me get you a birthday drink. What do you want?"

"How about an Old Fashioned?"

"You got it."

Just then, a hand tapped my shoulder from behind me and a female voice said, "Happy birthday, Jackson!"

I turned around to see who it was. When I came face to face to her, I froze in place and quickly looked at Chloe from the corner of my eyes.

I stood there, temporarily paralyzed by shock as Amber wrapped her arms around me and kissed me on the cheek, as Chloe watched from thirty feet away.

"Amber? Why are you here?" I asked as soon as I snapped out of it.

"I'm here for your birthday, silly." She touched my chest playfully.

"But who invited you?" Chloe asked as she came up next to me.

"I didn't tell you about my party," I added quickly to make it clear to Chloe that I had nothing to do with this.

Amber beamed at us. "Don't be embarrassed that you forgot to put my invitation in the mail. I came with Bruce, Jackson's co-worker. We're working on a deal together and he mentioned it during a work lunch the other week."

"Bruce," I repeated, making a mental note to give Bruce a piece of mind when I see him next.

"Well, it's good to see you two."

Amber's eyes moved from me to Chloe and then back to me. "Ahhh. Don't tell me you two are an item?" Then she laughed.

"What's your problem, Amber? Chloe and I have been together for awhile and I'm crazy about her. Are we back in first grade when you were jealous of her because I liked her and not you?"

"Relax, Jackson. You know I'm engaged." She laughed as she held out her left hand to show off the large diamond on her ring finger. "I have nothing to be jealous of."

I glared at Amber and for the first time, I saw what Chloe had been saying all along. I finally saw Amber's true colors.

Chapter Twelve

CHLOE

I was still upset when I went to the restroom after our encounter with Amber. I didn't know why she had that effect on me, and I didn't like the jealous and angry person that came out of me when she was around.

I stared at myself in the mirror in the restroom and tried to remind myself that she didn't matter, that I was better than her and needed to rise above the pettiness.

"We are adults now, Chloe," I said to my reflection. "You have Jax, the guy you want to be with for the rest of your life. She can't touch that. She has nothing on you now."

Feeling a lot better, I went into one of the stalls. But just as I locked the stall door behind me, I heard a familiar voice as the bathroom door opened.

"Steph, so I'm at this bar for Jackson's birthday—yes, *the* Jackson completely-fuckable Pierce!" Amber started to giggle. "Right? So hot!"

It was Amber on a call with Steph. I knew that name well. Steph was one of Amber's minions in their "mean girl" clique.

I was about to unlock the stall door and break up their conversation, but stopped myself when I heard her say my name.

"Anyway, guess who's also here? No, guess. Dirty Girl Chloe!" Amber started laughing hysterically. "Can you believe Jackson's with her, of all people? Gag me now. Ugh. I mean, it's no wonder though. I mean, now that I'm finally off the market, he's finally hit rock bottom."

At that point, I couldn't stand it any longer. I opened the door and walked out of the stall.

For a brief second, Amber's eyes grew wide when she saw me through the reflection. But she recovered quickly and a smirk appeared on her face.

"Steph, I'll call you back," she said before hanging up the phone.

"You're such a fucking bitch, Amber."

She just smiled and looked me up and down. "Wow, Chloe. This is a new low for you."

I glared at her. "What are you talking about?"

"Well I was having a private conversation just now. But you obviously stayed in that bathroom stall so you can eavesdrop on me." She pursed her lips and shook her head with disappointment. "Didn't your parents teach you any manners?" Then her expression changed, like she'd just remembered something. "Oh yeah, that's right, you didn't have any parents to teach you anything."

My jaw tightened and I clenched my fist into a ball, I felt my nails digging into my palm. Then I unclenched my fist and slowly drew in a deep breath to calm myself. I needed to keep my composure. I knew she was trying to get me upset and I didn't want her to have the satisfaction. Besides, this was Jackson's birthday party and all of his friends were here. I didn't want to cause a scene and have this be their memory of the night.

"Why are you such an unhappy person, Amber? Don't you have better things to do than to call a friend and tell her about me? Am I that important in your life?" I flashed Amber one of her signature bitch-smiles. "Do I threaten you *that* much?"

"*You* threaten me?" She snorted. "Pst, please."

"Then why do you do it? Why do you put in so much effort to try to put me down? Have you realized that in all these years, it's never really worked?"

"That's simple. I enjoy it. It's fun. It amuses me."

"Why?" I couldn't help but ask, trying to figure out why Amber had it out for me.

"You know, Chloe. For as long as I've known you, you've always seemed to like other people's used goods—hand-me-downs. Like those dirty overalls you used to wear all the time with those cigarette burns on them. It's like you *like* other people's trash. So Jackson is perfect for you, seeing as I fucked him before you did. To me, he's just used goods. You're basically just getting my leftovers." She started giggling as she touched up her lipstick in the mirror. "Oh, and you know that thing he does with his hips, right before he comes in you—that twist. Well that number was all me. I taught him that." She glanced at me through the mirror and smiled. "You're welcome."

That was the final straw for me. Before I knew what I was doing, I yanked her hair back and punched her in the face, aiming right at her nose.

She screamed out in pain and fell back. As blood started running down her nose, she ran toward the bathroom door. "You crazing fucking bitch! I think you broke my nose!"

Just then, Jackson rushed into the bathroom. "I heard a scream. Clo, are you okay?" He ran to my side.

"I'm fine," I huffed as I felt the adrenaline speed through my veins.

"Jackson," Amber yelled back from the doorway. "Your girlfriend is fucking crazy. You need to control her. She's like some rabid dog that needs to be put down."

I saw Jackson's body tighten and eyes narrow, and I grabbed his hand to calm him down. The last thing I wanted was to get Jackson arrested for assaulting a woman because of me.

Jackson shot a cold glare at Amber and snorted. "Amber, my girlfriend is just the right amount of crazy for me. And let's be honest, you probably deserved it."

"You two deserve each other!" she screamed as she ran out of the bathroom. "Crazy fucking people!"

"Are you okay?" Jackson looked at my hand, which was red around the knuckles.

I smiled. "More than okay." I rubbed my hand. "It hurts now, but that was so worth it."

He laughed and wrapped his arms around me. "I guess all those years of me being your punching bag has really paid off."

I giggled and punched him gently. "I guess I should thank you for that, huh?"

A devious smirk curled his lips. "I believe it's time you paid your dues." Suddenly, he grabbed my hand and led me out of the bathroom, down the hallway, and into a dark coat room.

I shrieked with glee, feeling a rush of excitement as we moved deep into the back of the coatroom.

"Baby, you've been killing me in that skin-tight dress," his deep, raspy voice came from behind me. "I can't wait until we get home anymore. You've been driving me crazy all night." His lips moved gently down the side of my neck as he wrapped his arms around my waist.

"Jax," I gasped, unable to resist his touch.

I rubbed my body up against him and felt his already-rock-hard erection against my back.

"Do you feel how hard I am for you already?" he groaned into my ear and the heat of his breath sent a shiver down my body.

"Yes," I moaned as I felt a pool of wetness collect between my legs. "But..." I gasped, trying to focus on my words, "But shouldn't we go out to your party? All your friends and colleagues are there buying you birthday drinks." Then I suddenly cried out in pleasure as I felt his hand between my legs.

"Fuck, I love it when you wear dresses. It—," he groaned as he thrusted his erection against my back, "—makes it so easy for me to touch you." Without warning, he entered me with two fingers, causing me to gasp as I lost all control of myself. My muscles clenched onto his fingers as waves of pleasure rippled through my body.

"We *could* go back out to the party and drink with my friends," he said in a deep, husky voice, "but it's my birthday, and do you want to know what I'd rather be drinking right now?"

"W—what?" I panted, as his fingers moved in and out of me.

"I'd rather be drinking that sweet, wet honey that I just can't get enough of and it's right here, and it's all mine." He drove his fingers deep inside my wetness, and I felt myself spasm around his hands.

Suddenly, he removed his fingers and turned me around to face him. I inhaled sharply as I felt his fingers, still wet from my juices, slowly brush the spaghetti straps of my dress off my shoulders, causing the silk fabric to fall to the ground, exposing my naked breasts.

"Damn, I've been craving these all night," he groaned as he lowered his mouth onto one of my breasts and began to suck on it.

Then he grabbed my waist and in one swift movement, he laid me down on top of a bed of coats. Within seconds, I felt his teeth and tongue bite and soothe my nipples in alternating intervals, sending jolts of electricity down below where a pool of wetness began to develop.

"Now that I've got you all wet and excited, I'm ready for my birthday drink from you, baby."

Knowing exactly what he had in store for me, the wetness inside me began to drip down my thighs in anticipation.

As if he had a sixth sense of how turned on I was, he went down on his knees and disappeared between my legs.

I gasped as I felt his hot tongue lick up my wetness along my inner thigh. "Can't let this sweetness go to waste," he groaned as his mouth slowly moved toward my entrance. "And happy fucking birthday to me," His voice was ragged and wild as I felt his mouth linger at the entrance.

"Oh God, please, Jax!" I begged as I arched my hips toward his mouth.

"Baby, you know I can't deny you anything," he growled. He grabbed my hips with both hands as his mouth engulfed me. I screamed out and threw my head back as a flood of pleasure crashed through me. As his hands tightened their grip against my flesh and he pulled me against his mouth, his tongue moved deeper and deeper inside me. Within seconds, I reached my breaking point and my entire body began to convulse around his mouth.

"Come in my mouth, baby. I want to get drunk off of your wet pussy."

I cried and gasped uncontrollably as his tongue worked its magic and pushed me over the brink of sanity, and for five long seconds, earth-shattering pleasure thundered through my body.

"Oh my God. That was incredible," I panted.

"And delicious to the last drop." He moved up from between my legs and kissed me slowly, allowing me to taste myself all over his mouth.

"And we're not done, birthday boy," I purred. I grabbed his shoulders and rolled him to his back and got on top of him.

I kissed him softly up his jaw line and nibbled his ear. "I'm going to ride you until you come deep inside me, baby. Are you ready?"

"Fuck yeah," he groaned as I felt his pelvic thrust up in response.

I pulled down his pants and boxers and his long, hard erection sprung out to greet me. I grabbed the base of his shaft and took the entire length of his cock into my mouth in one slow and fluid motion.

He let out a primal groan as his hips moved up to thrust deeper inside my mouth. I moved my mouth up and down his erection until I felt his body start to spasm in pleasure. That was when I stopped and pulled out.

"That was just to get you warmed up, Jax," I moaned. "Now I want to ride you like a cowgirl, and baby, I like my rides rough and fast."

"God, you're killing me, baby," he panted.

"Do you want to punish me for torturing you?"

Before he could answer, I mounted him, easing his cock deep inside me. We cried out together as I began to ride his cock, first slowly as I moved up and down his entire length, my pussy clung tightly around him as I moved. Then, with each thrust inside me, I moved my hips faster and harder up and down his shaft until I felt him lose control of his body.

"Oh, baby. I'm about to fucking come," he warned.

"Just let go, Jax. Just lose yourself inside me," I cried as I felt myself spasm around him. "I'm coming, Jax," I panted. "Baby, I'm coming with you."

And we did. Moments later, as our bodies moved in perfect harmony, we both found our release. As I collapsed on top of him, our bodies still connected, I let out a deep sigh of satisfaction.

"Happy birthday, Jax," I whispered as we laid there on top of a bed of coats.

"Thank you, baby."

"Have you made your birthday wish today?"

He caressed my face. "No need, Clo. It's already come true."

As I felt his lips kiss me tenderly on my forehead, I wrapped my arms around his warm, toned chest and sank a little deeper into him.

This is true bliss, I thought to myself. *This is the epitome of happiness.*

Chapter Thirteen

JACKSON

"Hey, babe. How's packing going?"

I heard Chloe moan. "Well if you would just tell me where we're going, it'd really make life a little easier."

"Well I did say to pack one set of suitcases for a tropical weather vacation and then pack another set of suitcases for a winter weather vacation. It's not that hard."

"You're basically asking me to just divide up my closet in half and pack it all," she protested.

I laughed. "Well, no, that's probably not a good idea. You don't need to bring that much clothes with you. It's only for a week."

"Jaaaax," she whined. "Come on! Just tell me where we're going so I'm not packing like a blind person."

"But then it wouldn't be a surprise trip then, would it?" I couldn't stop smiling, thinking about the surprise vacation I had planned for us.

"Pretty please, Jax? You're picking me up in like four hours for the airport. I'll find out at the airport when we get our boarding passes, so why don't you just tell me know. It's already the date of the trip, so it'll still be a surprise if you tell me know. Pllllease?"

I shook my head but finally gave in. "Fine. Fine. Fine. You're right. It's been a surprise for the last two weeks since I first told you about it. I guess since we're leaving in a few hours, I should save you the trouble of packing all those tropical clothes."

"We're going somewhere cold?" she asked, quickly picking up my clue.

"Yup."

"Tell me!"

"Okay. I'm taking you to Finland…specifically the Kakslauttanen Arctic Resort!"

"Oh my God," she squealed into the phone. "Are you serious?"

I laughed and heard some rustling on her end. "Are you jumping up and down right now, or am I hearing things?"

The rustling stopped. "I will not confirm nor deny that," she tried to say flatly, causing me to laugh harder.

"So are we really going to Kakslauttanen? Like really?" she asked in disbelief.

"Yup, I'm taking you to see the Aurora Borealis so you can check that off of your bucket list."

"Jax, you're the best." I could hear the emotion in her voice. "I can't believe you still remember that from my bucket list. It told you that when we were thirteen."

"Are you crying already?" I teased.

"I will not confirm nor deny that," she responded.

"You know? You're just too cute sometimes."

"And that's why you love me," she replied, her voice filled with excitement.

"That's one of the many reasons."

"Oh! Are we going to be staying in the glass igloos like in the photo I have?"

"What do you think?"

"Yes!"

"Well, you think right then." I grinned from ear to ear as I tried to picture how cute she must look right now. She always looked beautiful when she was deliriously happy.

"Jax, I seriously can't wait. I'm so lucky to have an incredible boyfriend like you!"

"Flattery is always welcomed here," I said with a chuckle. My chest felt full, knowing how happy she was at this moment, knowing I was the one that made that happen.

"Do you know what I'm doing now, Jax?"

"What, babe?"

"I'm pinching myself right now to make sure I'm not dreaming this."

I threw my head back in laughter. "You're too cute, silly girl. I love you."

"Aww, Jax. I love you, too. You have no idea how happy you've made me."

"Well I'm sure you'll find a way to show me."

"Oh, you know I will," she promised seductively.

Three hours later, it was two o'clock, and I was leaving work early for the trip. I hailed a cab and headed home to pick up Chloe and our luggage. When I got into the cab, I started responding to some afternoon work emails.

Then the office called. It was Nick.

"Hey, Nick. What's going on?"

"Did you leave yet, Jackson?"

"Yeah, I just left."

"Shit. We need to get some filings in tonight with the SEC. Do you remember where you put the 2014 Financial Statements for ALD Inc.?"

"I have it somewhere in my email. I can forward that to you when we hang up."

"Okay, thanks, Jackson. Have a great time in Finland. Should we expect a special announcement when you guys get back?"

I frowned. "What are you talking about?"

"Like an engagement? Isn't that why you're taking her to this special place on her bucket list?"

"Nick, you're thinking too much into it. It's only been nine months since we started dating. We're taking things slow."

"Okay, that's cool, man. Julie asked me to ask."

I shook my head. "You're like Julie's puppet sometimes."

He laughed. "Are you saying you're not Chloe's?"

"Touché. Alright man, I'll send over the financial statement. Call or email me if the office needs anything from me. I should have some reception in Finland."

When I hung up with Nick, I saw the driver look at me through his rearview mirror.

I pulled up my email and start searching for the document Nick needed.

"You sound really busy, mister."

"Yeah," I responded absentmindedly as I scanned through my emails for the file. *Just my luck to get a talkative cab driver.*

"You got a girlfriend?"

I narrowed my eyes as I looked at the back of his head. *That's a little nosy.*

"You know," he continued despite my silence, "Today I went to my doctor to get the results of my annual health exam."

I glanced up quickly at him, wondering why he couldn't tell I wasn't interested in talking at the moment. I continued to scan through my emails for the file.

"It's colon cancer," the driver continued, but now, I wasn't ignoring his words anymore. He let out a heavy sigh.

"Suddenly I started to think about whether there were any regrets in my life. I'm worried that I won't have enough time to say 'thank you' to my parents for everything they've done for me in my life." I noticed a black and white photo of a couple taped on the middle console above the air vent.

"I'm worried that I won't have enough time to say 'I love you' one more time to my wife and hold her in my arms." I noticed another photo above the air vent—a wedding photo of who I assume was the driver and his wife.

"I'm also worried that I won't have enough time to see my child grow up." I notice a third picture taped on the middle console. It was a proud father with a wide and infectious grin on his face as he held his new born baby.

The driver let out another heavy sigh. "I had to wait until the countdown of my life to realize that it's probably too late for many things in my life."

I felt my body stiffen as I glanced over at the driver's photo ID badge secured behind the front passenger seat. He looked like he wasn't any older than I was.

"You know, sometimes we really have to stop and give ourselves more time to do the things we want to do. Because one day when you least expect it, we start wondering if we have any regrets, and by then, we're worried that it's already too late to do everything we'd wanted to accomplish in our lives."

His words struck a chord with me, and instead of going back home, I told the driver that I needed to make a detour before heading home.

Chapter Fourteen

JACKSON

It was a lengthy trip from Philadelphia to the Kakslauttanen Arctic Resort, which was located within the arctic circle of northern Finland. After a flight into Helsinki, the capital of Finland, we had to take another flight into the closest city and then a thirty-minute shuttle through the mountainous region of northern Finland to get to the resort.

But when we finally arrived at this resort that was situated in the middle of the snow-covered wilderness, I knew instantly why this place had been on Chloe's bucket list since she read about it when we were growing up.

"This place feels like a fairy tale," Chloe gasped as we stepped out of the shuttle, expressing exactly how I was feeling as I looked around in awe at how enchanting everything looked around us.

Chloe let out a squeal of excitement as we collected our luggage.

"You're so cute sometimes." I kissed her nose. As gust of snow flurries blew past us, I examined her snow parka to make sure it was tightly wrapped around her.

"Jax, this is the best surprise I can ever imagine." She beamed up at me, her eyes twinkled with excitement. "You're the best." She put her arms around my neck and pulled me down for a kiss.

"I know," I agreed as she pulled away. "I really am."

She giggled, but didn't bother to hit my chest playfully like she normally would when I made an obnoxious comment—she was too excited to be here to even bother.

"What are you most excited about?" I asked her as we headed into the resort with our luggage. "Besides the aurora borealis, or course, which they say we'll be able to see all week here."

She looked up at me and beamed—this delirious happiness that seemed to exude from every facet of her being. "Promise you won't laugh."

I chuckled at her request. "Well if you put it like that, I'm pretty sure I won't be able to keep that promise."

She made a face at me. "You're the worst at promises."

"I am, aren't I?"

I knew she was teasing, but she was right—almost every promise I've made her, I've broken. As much as that saddened me, I knew it only pushed me harder to make it up to her.

"So I'm really excited to see Santa's Home."

I tried to hold back my laughter. "You know Santa's not real, right?" I teased her.

She made a face at me. "I knew you'd laugh."

"You know me so well." I snickered. "So why are you most excited about seeing Santa's Home here?"

"Well I've never been to the arctic circle, and probably won't ever be back. I know he's not real, but when I grew up, I really believed in him. My mom told me he gave me the Belle Barbie doll I got one year. I used to think if Santa gave me the Belle for Christmas, that meant he saw that I was a good girl, and maybe one year, if I was really good, he'd help my mom get better. That was always the top present I'd always wished for each year."

I pulled her into my arms and held her. "You are the most incredible person I know, Clo," I whispered. "I'm so lucky to have you in my life." My heart went out to her. I knew she'd had a hard life growing up, her innocence stripped from her before she even knew what it was. Her life had always been about sacrifice and compassion for those around her, for those she loved—and she would give her all to those she cared for, willingly and without hesitation.

"Come on, let's go visit Santa's Home. Then we can go on the reindeer ride."

She giggled. "That's actually the second thing I was looking forward to the most."

I swung my arms around her. "Don't I know you well?"

"Jax. Thanks for bringing me here and making this dream come true." She looked up at me with an innocent gleam of delight in her eyes. It was a look I'd rarely seen in her, and it touched me knowing that I helped put it there. So to see this sheer joy in her eyes, the glimpse of unadulterated innocence took my breath away.

❦ ❦ ❦

We turned the lights off in the room, and the magical green glow of the aurora borealis moved across the sky like fast-moving colorful clouds as they cast the only light in our small glass igloo.

"God, Jax, isn't this just amazing?" She looked up at the sky in awe, taking in one of the oldest places that'd been on her bucket list of places to see in her lifetime.

"It's incredible," I agreed, half looking up at the northern lights and half looking at her. She was a vision of beauty and I knew this was the moment—the perfect one. Palms sweaty, I pulled out the smooth velvet container that'd weighed down in my pant pockets since we left New York.

"There are just no words," she continued, her voice full of bliss as she took in the wide expanse of the sky overhead. "The moving colors, the thousands of bright stars, and that brilliant glow across the black night. The picture on the clipping in the *Discover* magazine I've kept of this place doesn't do this justice. It's—"

"Enchanting," I finished for her as I bent down on one knee, my eyes locked onto her—the most enchanting thing before me.

"Yeah, enchanting," she repeated dreamily.

"Clo," I said as I looked up at her, waiting for her to look back at me. I heard a nervousness in my voice that I hope she hadn't noticed.

"Yeah?" she asked absentmindedly as she glanced back at me quickly.

A grin spread across my face as I watched how cute she looked during that split-second of confusion when she didn't see me standing in front of her like I had moments before. I couldn't express in words how amazing it felt to watch that confusion turn to understanding on her beautiful face as she lowered her head to look down toward me.

Then I pressed the small remote in my other hand, which turned on a portable stereo, and a second later, "Truly Madly Deeply" by Savage Garden started playing softly in the background.

"I know how much you loved this song when we were in high school," I whispered.

She nodded, her eyes wide and wet with emotion as she met my gaze. Her mouth opened and then closed, but no sound came out.

I beamed up at her, trying to savor this moment in my mind, trying to memorize it so I could always return to it. I held up the velvet box in front of her and slowly opened it, revealing the vintage ring inside.

She gasped. I could see the nerves, wonderment, and excitement across her face—the same feelings I was feeling inside as I looked up at her—at my best friend, my love, and—hopefully—my soon-to-be wife.

"Jax," she let out in a hushed voice, "That looks like the ring from Doyle & Doyle in New York when we went nine months ago."

"It *is* the ring from Doyle & Doyle." I beamed up at her, remembering how much she had loved this ring that day.

She looked like she was in shock as she looked down at the engagement ring in disbelief. "But how were you able to get it? Didn't they say that it was a really rare vintage diamond ring and expected it to be sold by the end of that week?"

"It *was* sold by the end of that week—actually end of that day." My grin grew wider as I saw the understanding flash through her eyes.

"You didn't," she gasped.

I nodded. "I went back later that day and bought it. I knew then that this day would come and I wanted to give you the perfect ring. It looked beautiful on you, and I knew from the way your face lit up when you put it on that it made you happy."

"You've had it this entire time?" She was still in disbelief. "But we've been living together. I've never seen it before around the house or in the safety deposit box you have in the bedroom."

I chuckled. "Do you really think I'd risk spoiling the surprise and miss out on this priceless look on your face? It's been sitting in my safety deposit box at the bank."

"Oh." She became silent when she finally accepted that this ring was really in front of her. "It's beautiful, Jax," she whispered. "It's *too* beautiful." There were tears in her eyes as she stared between the ring and then to me.

"It was made for you, Clo. To me, you're like this ring—you're a rare, one-of-a-kind diamond that could never be replicated."

"Oh, Jax. I…" Tears streamed down her face. "I don't know what to say."

"Just say yes." I reached for her hand. "I love you, Clo. When we were thirteen, we made a pact under the makeshift northern lights I created on your bedroom ceiling. I promised you that night that I'd marry you and be there for you. Now that I have you in my life, now that I know how happy I can be with you by my side, I realize that that promise isn't enough for me anymore. With this ring, and under the real aurora borealis, I promise you a forever. I promise you my now, my forever, and everything in between. Will you let me fulfill this promise to you and marry me?"

"Yes." She threw her arms around me and pressed her lips on mine. "Yes. Yes. Yes," she repeated when she pulled away, her voice softer each time she repeated it. I slipped the ring onto her finger and it still fit perfectly, like it was made just for her.

Chapter Fifteen

CHLOE

"You're kidding, right?" Jackson looked up from his Calculus textbook.

I giggled and shook my head. "No, I'm serious. I love this place." I leaned back against the palm of my hands and inhaled the subtle, sweet smell of freshly cut grass. "Wouldn't you want to have yours here?"

"I've actually never thought about where I'd want to get married." He looked around at the lake. "I do love this place, but it never crossed my mind."

I smiled as I looked over at the bridge at the narrow end of the lake and saw a small glare reflecting off of something on the bridge. I knew it was our love lock. When the afternoon sun hit its shiny, metal surface at just the right angle, it would always give off a glare, reminding me that it was there.

"I think this place is perfect. It's one of my favorite places and I've had a lot of great memories here."

"So you don't want a fancy wedding?"

I shook my head. "Nothing is important except how happy I'd be at my wedding. I know I'd be happy here. None of that other stuff matters."

❧ ❧ ❧

"Are you nervous?" Uncle Tom gave me a reassuring smile as he offered his arm.

I looked up into his gaze and smiled confidently "No. I've never been more ready about anything in my life."

Uncle Tom patted my hand and smiled back knowingly, "Your Aunt and I have always known you two were destined to be together, even when you were just a couple of kids splashing around in this very lake."

We both turned and stared out at the lake, now decorated for my wedding. It was the perfect place to hold a summer wedding, with the tall, leafy trees providing a natural canopy of shade and the clear blue water shimmering in the sunlight. The sound of birds singing provided the ideal background music. And all the summer flowers were in bloom, filling the air with fragrant smells.

It wasn't the breathtaking beauty of the lake that made me want to hold my wedding there though; it was the special place it would always hold in my heart. This was the place where Jackson and I had spent so much time together growing up. This was the place where we sealed our promise to marry each other with our love lock. This was the place where we first felt something deeper for each other than mere friendship.

I smiled as we heard the swelling of music from the string quartet as they started to play Pachelbel's *Canon in D*. Taking a deep breath for courage, Uncle

Tom and I pushed through the privacy curtain and walked slowly down the path.

The clearing by the lake had been completely transformed into an enchanted garden. A lattice arch had been set up at the far end of the path completely covered in tulips, pink peonies and apricot pink English roses—all my favorites. Jackson had asked if he could be in charge of selecting the flowers for the ceremony and I was impressed that he had remembered.

Twinkling white lights strung everywhere through the trees, giving the woods a magical quality like something from a dream.

White folding chairs covered in tulle and fresh flowers had been set up on both sides of the arch with an aisle going right down the middle. Jackson stood just to the right of it, looking incredibly handsome in a black tuxedo with an apricot pink English rosebud in his lapel.

Everyone stood and gasped in awe as I started to walk slowly down the aisle clinging to Uncle Tom's arm. As I felt their eyes upon me and heard their oohs and ahhs, I felt truly beautiful for the first time in my life, like a fairytale bride floating on a magical cloud.

My dress was a simple design made by Vera Wang. The sleeveless bodice was made of embroidered lace accented with tiny pearls and the flowing skirt was comprised of layers of silk organza that cascaded over my body like a waterfall. My hair hung loose down my back in soft curls, topped with a crown of delicate flowers on my head.

As I walked down the endless aisle toward Jackson, all I could see was him as the rest of the world faded into the background. We smiled at each other, our eyes never leaving the other as I walked toward him.

When we reached the end of the aisle, Uncle Tom kissed my cheek and gazed into my eyes one last time. He was the only father figure I had ever really known and I saw the pride and love he felt for me in that moment and knew that I was like a daughter in his heart. We hugged each other tightly but briefly before he gently handed my hand over to Jackson.

To Jackson, he whispered, "Take care of her."

Jackson nodded. "Always."

When we stood there, holding each others' hands, I saw the sheer happiness and joy in his eyes—the same I'd felt inside.

"And now the couple will exchange rings and say aloud the special vows they have each prepared," the Officiate said as he smiled between me and Jackson.

This was the moment I had been dreaming about all my life, and it was suddenly happening with the man of my dreams.

Jackson took the platinum band we had picked out together and slid it onto my left hand where it nestled perfectly against the breathtaking vintage engagement ring.

I saw him draw in a deep breath to steady himself. He looked into my eyes and smiled that boyish grin I'd fallen madly in love with.

"My dearest Clo, I have so many things I want to say to you right now, but all my thousands of words can be merged into one sentence: Thank you for appearing in my life, for forgiving me for my mistakes, for allowing me to spend the rest of my life trying to make you as happy as you've made me. I love you so much, and I promise to do everything in my power, for the rest of my days, to make you as happy as you made me on the day you agreed to be my bride."

I saw the tears in his eyes as he finished his vows, and I swallowed hard against the lumps of emotion that were caught in my throat. All I wanted to do was throw myself into his arms right then and kiss him, but I resisted the temptation.

I slipped the platinum wedding band onto his broad finger and tried to blink back the tears that threatened to break free from my eyes.

Then, in front of all our friends and loved ones, I froze. I had written a speech I wanted to say to Jackson in front of everyone I loved and cared about, but at that moment, it had suddenly disappeared from my mind.

I started to panic, but then, as if he knew what I was thinking, I felt him squeeze my hands and I met his gaze. At that moment, all my nervousness melted away, and as I got lost in his warm, emerald eyes, the words that expressed everything I felt for him came out.

"Jax, since as early as I can remember, I always wanted to feel loved, to feel wanted, and feel safe. There's no other place I feel more loved and safe than within your arms. You've loved me when I felt unlovable and you've loved me when I didn't feel like I deserved it. Thank you. Thank you for being the very best friend I could ever hope for. Thank you for coming into my life."

I saw the emotion well up in Jackson's eyes and I knew my vow had touched his heart the same way his had touched mine.

"I now pronounce you husband and wife. You may now kiss the bride," the Officiant declared.

Jackson didn't even wait for him to finish the sentence before he pulled me into his strong arms and kissed me passionately, stealing my breath away as I melted into his embrace.

JACKSON

"Well, we did it, Mrs. Pierce." I grinned at Chloe and watched her eyes light up when she heard me call her by her married name for the first time.

"We sure did, Mr. Pierce." Chloe smiled back at me and kissed me.

I had always known that Chloe was beautiful, but when she was walking toward me down the aisle at the lake, I was blown away by how stunning she looked. Her face was glowing, her eyes were like gemstones, and her smile had never been lovelier. It had taken all my restraint not to run toward her and sweep her into my arms.

The reception hall was located fairly close to the lake and all our friends and family were already there by the time we'd finished getting our pictures taken with the photographer by the lake.

"Congratulations! I trust you'll take good care of our girl." I felt a friendly tap on my shoulder and I turned to face Chloe's Uncle Tom and Aunt Betty, both of whom were grinning broadly.

"I promise." I gave Uncle Tom a hearty handshake, but Aunt Betty insisted on a hug.

"I'm still going to cook extra food for you, so whenever you need a hot meal just come and visit us. You don't even need to call first," Aunt Betty said.

I stood back as Chloe hugged Aunt Betty and Uncle Tom while they gushed about the ceremony. Then Chloe looked around anxiously and asked, "Where's Charlie? I hope the ceremony wasn't too much for him and he had to leave."

"Are you kidding?" Aunt Betty said with a laugh. "We can't get that boy to take it easy now that he's in love. Ever since he's met Kendra, nothing is too much for him anymore." Aunt Betty laughed heartily and jerked her head in the direction of the dance floor.

We all looked to find Charlie dancing exuberantly in his wheelchair, popping wheelies and spinning in circles with a lovely girl, who was laughing and smiling as she twirled around him. I glanced at Chloe and saw the look of relief in her eyes just before they started to fill with tears of joy. I knew how deep her feelings ran about her cousin's accident and I hoped seeing him look so happy and healthy would finally put her guilt at ease and give her the peace she deserved.

As the D.J. got ready to play a new song, I held my hand to Chloe, bowed with exaggerated chivalry and said, "You know, Mrs. Pierce, we haven't had our first dance as husband and wife yet. What do say Clo, shall we?"

"It's about time. I thought you'd never ask." She grinned at me playfully and followed me to the dance floor. I nodded at the D.J. and he put on the record I had specifically requested.

As "At Last" by Etta James filled the air, I held Chloe close into my arms as we moved through the dance floor.

"I love you, Clo," I whispered in her ear. "Whenever you look at me, I see everything I know I'll ever need in life. I'm so thankful that this day has finally arrived."

"I love you too, Jax." She looked up at me with tear-filled eyes. "You've made me happier than I ever thought was possible for me."

"Baby, I know it took us some time to get here. When we were thirteen, I promised to marry you when we turned thirty," I said as I gazed into her eyes. "I'm sorry I'm about two years late."

"No, Jax." She smiled up at me and pulled my head down to her. And just before our lips met in a long, tender kiss, she whispered, "You're just on time."

Epilogue

JACKSON

One Year Later

"How did a year pass us by so quickly?"

"Because we're so happy. Time flies when people are happy." She looked over at me with a smile as we walked the familiar path next to the lake that held so many memories for us.

Chloe stopped when we got to the middle of the bridge, and I looked at the love lock that was secured to the railing.

"Can you believe it's been here for fourteen years?" I held the lock and flipped it over to see the inscription I'd had etched on the back:

Jax & Clo
June 2003
Unbreakable Friendship & Love.
Promise to Marry in 2014.

"I know. You were right, Jax." She met my gaze and a smile appeared on her pink lips.

"I know I'm usually right," I teased, "But what am I am right about this time?"

"When you got this love lock as a present to me for our high school graduation, you said that there was this belief that if two people lock a love lock against the railing of a bridge and then throw away the keys, it's supposed to symbolize unbreakable love." She grinned. "I think we've proved that belief right. We've gone through so many obstacles since we'd put this lock here, but despite everything, our love remained strong and unbreakable."

My chest filled with happiness as I took in her words. "I love you, Mrs. Pierce," I said as I lowered my mouth and kissed her.

"I love you, too, Mr. Pierce."

Then I remembered something. "So what is this anniversary gift that you're so confident will be better than the one I got you?" I flashed her a doubtful smirk.

She grinned in silence like she was amused by the secret she was keeping. "Ye of little faith." She made a tsk tsk sound with her tongue. "Mr. Pierce, you should know by now that your wife is always right."

I chuckled and pulled her into my embrace again as I let the word, "wife" linger in my thoughts. I could never grow tired of hearing her tell me she was mine. As I inhaled her intoxicating scent, I whispered, "Mrs. Pierce, you should know by now that your husband is very stubborn to admit things even when he knows his wife is right."

She giggled and rolled her eyes.

"So where's my anniversary gift," I playfully demanded.

"It's this," she said with a knowing smile as she handed me a small, heavy box."

I looked at her. "I'm pretty sure my gift to you will be better—it's certainly bigger."

She laughed. "Bigger doesn't mean better."

"You've never had any complaints," I teased.

She hit me across my chest, and I pretended to wince in pain.

"Now open the box and you'll find out that my gift is better."

"Fine." I opened the box as she watched me with amusement.

When I saw what was inside, I looked up at Chloe in surprise. "It can't be," I exclaimed. If this was what I thought it was, then she was right, this anniversary gift was better than mine—much better.

"Take it out," she urged. "Let's put it against the railing and throw away the keys. I want to make sure this will be an unbreakable love."

I was filled with so much emotion, I couldn't speak. I reached for the love lock from the box. We both secured it together against the railing. As soon as we threw the keys into the lake, I grabbed her into my arms.

"Clo, I never thought I could be any happier than the day you married me, but today, you proved me wrong. You've made me the happiest man on earth for a second time."

As we walked back home to share the news with Aunt Betty and Uncle Tom, a new shiny love lock was now next to the one that we'd placed there fourteen years ago. On the back of this new love lock was the inscription:

Jax, Clo & Baby
July 2017
Unbreakable Love & Family
Expected Arrival in February 2018

The End

Author's Note

Thank you for reading *Promise of Forever*, book three in the three-book series *Promises*. I hope you've enjoyed Chloe and Jackson's love story.

Please consider telling your friends and leaving a review for this book. As an indie author, word of mouth and reviews help other readers to discovery my works.

Other Books

If you would like to stay informed of new releases, teasers, and news on my upcoming books, please sign up for Jessica Wood's mailing list or visit me at my website:

http://jessicawoodauthor.com/mailing-list/

http://jessicawoodauthor.com

Emma's Story Series

- *A Night to Forget* – Book One
- *The Day to Remember* – Book Two
- *Emma's Story* Box Set – Contains Book One & Book Two

The Heartbreaker Series

This is an *Emma's Story* spin-off series featuring Damian Castillo, a supporting character in *The Day to Remember*. This is a standalone series and does not need to be read with *Emma's Story* series.

- *Damian* – Book One
- *The Heartbreaker* – Prequel Novella to *DAMIAN* – can be read before or after *Damian.*
- *Taming Damian* – Book Two
- *The Heartbreaker Box Set* – Contains all three books.

The Chase Series

This is a standalone series with cameo appearances from Damian Castillo (*The Heartbreaker series*).

- *The Chase, Vol. 1*
- *The Chase, Vol. 2*
- *The Chase, Vol. 3*
- *The Chase, Vol. 4*
- *The Chase: The Complete Series Box Set* – Contains All Four Volumes

Oblivion

This is a standalone full-length book unrelated to other series by Jessica Wood.

- *Oblivion* (Synopsis & Exclusive Excerpt below)

Promises Series

This is a standalone series unrelated to other series by Jessica Wood.

- *Promise to Marry* – *Book One*
- *Promise to Keep* – *Book Two*
- *Promise of Forever* – *Book Three*

***

Pre-Orders Currently Available

Contracted Love – June 30, 2015 **(Synopsis below)**

***

Contracted Love – Synopsis

We met in the dark as strangers, had sex by mistake, and married each other to hide a secret.

We both agreed it'd be a marriage of convenience, to fix the mess we had gotten ourselves in the day we met.

But when it was time to get an annulment, my feelings had changed. I wanted more. I wanted to stay by his side. But did he want the same?

Contracted Love **is a completely standalone full-length book and is currently available on pre-order.**

Oblivion – Synopsis & Excerpt

SYNOPSIS

I wake up to a life and a man that I can't remember.

He says his name is Connor Brady—the tall, sexy CEO of Brady Global, Inc.

He says my name is Olivia Stuart, and that I was recently in an accident and lost my memory.

Also, he says I'm his fiancé.

Although I don't remember Connor, or anything about my past, something about him seems familiar. He is kind, protective, and breathtakingly-gorgeous. But there is just one problem—he seems *too* perfect.

As I begin to rebuild my relationship with Connor and accept the idea that I may never remember my past, I unexpectedly meet Ethan James.

Ethan is the mysterious, rebellious stranger who pushes my boundaries to their limits and makes me feel alive. As our lives collide time and time again, the bits and pieces of my past start to unravel, unearthing the secrets that have been buried deep inside my subconscious. With every new memory I gain about who I once was, I become more torn between the man who is my fiancé and the stranger who is the key to my past. Is my life with Connor really as perfect as he leads me to believe?

CHAPTER ONE

Tears streamed down my face as I ran into my bedroom and slammed the door behind me. I reached for my diary—the familiar pink leather journal that was filled with my deepest thoughts. My shaky fingers pulled the gold fabric ribbon page marker, taking me to my last entry, and I began to frantically scribble down everything I was feeling at that moment—all the pain and fear that raced inside me as the screaming escalated an octave higher between my parents outside of my room.

They're fighting again. It's been happening more and more frequently, each time worse than the day before.

I wish they weren't so unhappy. I wish my parents didn't hate each other so much. I wish I was anyone else but myself right now. I wish I was anywhere else but here.

As if hearing my thoughts, I heard my father roar, "If you want a fucking divorce, you can have it! But I'm going to warn you just this once: if you walk out of that door, don't ever think about coming back again!"

"I don't plan on it!" I heard my mother spit back. "I'm leaving first thing tomorrow, and I'm taking Liv with me!"

"No!" I cried, my mind racing as I thought about everything I was about to lose.

Just then, my room and the pink leather diary in my hand faded away into the background as my consciousness registered a soft, steady beeping in the distance. What is that?

When I turned toward the sound, I found myself running across a familiar street in the middle of the night. I was wearing a jewel-encrusted blush-pink evening gown that weighed down on my body and restricted my movement. The air was bitter cold and cutting, but the adrenaline that coursed inside me seemed to shelter me from the cold like a numbing blanket.

Suddenly, I saw two bright, blinding headlights coming toward me at high speed. The sharp screeching of car tires filled the air, drowning out all other noise. I felt the impact of cold metal against my body as I was lifelessly flung sideways against the solid pavement.

I braced myself for the impact of the pain that would greet my body.

But it didn't come.

Instead, the steady beeping returned, but this time, it seemed closer, louder.

Then a hushed conversation seeped through my consciousness.

"There's nothing we can do for her right now, Mr. Brady. As you know she has suffered some head injuries from the accident, so all we can do right now is to wait for her to wake up and see from there." The female voice seemed miles away, but for some reason, I knew she was talking about me.

"Okay. Thank you." The man's voice was strained and low as I heard him walk in my direction.

I felt my head throb in pain, in time with that unnerving beeping that became increasingly louder.

"She's very lucky to have someone like you to visit and be by her side every day. You must really care about her."

"Yeah. I do." The male voice was closer than before.

Then I felt a warm hand on mine, bringing me into the present. My mind registered the bed I was lying on. The smell of stale, chlorine air invaded my senses. The beeping came into focus and I could hear it coming from a machine a foot away from me. *Am I in a hospital?*

My fingers twitched as I tried to move my body.

"Nurse!" the man's voice cried out in alarm. "I think I felt her move."

My eyes fluttered open and closed, struggling against the heaviness of my lids and the blinding lights that stung my eyes.

"I think she's waking up!" The man squeezed my hand as he inched closer to my face. "Liv?"

"Mr. Brady, let's give her some room." The man loosened his grip on me and I heard him move away.

I opened my eyes again, and this time, it was easier. My vision was blurred as I looked around, but I could detect two figures close by.

"Ms. Stuart?" The female voice was gentle as she moved toward me.

"Where am I?" I blinked and after a couple of seconds, her face came into focus. "Who are you?" I looked around the room and found myself in a surprisingly large and luxurious hospital room.

"Ms. Stuart, you were in an accident and you're at The Pavilion, a private in-patient hospital unit at the University of Pennsylvania hospital. I'm Nurse Betty and I've been taking care of you."

"An accident." I repeated her words and tried to think through the dense fog consuming my every thought. Then I winced at the throbbing pain in my head.

"Are you in any pain?" She looked at me with concern.

"Just a horrible headache." I reached for my head.

"I'll let the doctor know and we'll get you something for that."

"What happened to me?" I looked up at her, searching her face for answers.

She flashed me a kind smile. "There's actually someone that's been here waiting for you to wake up for quite some time. I'll let him tell you what happened while I check your vitals." She moved aside and my eyes focused on the other figure in the room—the tall, handsome man in a tailored charcoal suit standing anxiously behind her.

"Hi." I looked at him, unsure of what else to say to this stranger.

"Liv? Thank God you finally woke up."

I smiled at him. His warm, hazel eyes were filled with concern as he moved in front of the nurse to grab my hand. I studied him, wondering why he seemed so familiar.

He reached for me. Deep creases formed between his brows as he furrowed them in worry. "Liv, how are you feeling?" His voice was smooth and gentle. I couldn't quite place where, but I knew I'd heard it before.

I placed my hands to my head and groaned. "Besides this killer headache, I'm okay." I tried to get up but my arms felt weak as I slumped back down against the pillows when I tried to sit up. He reached over and helped me lean up against the headboard of the bed.

"It's so good to see you awake." He held my face and kissed me gently on my forehead.

I flinched and frowned up at him. "Who are you? Have we met before?"

His expression changed immediately and he whipped around and turned to the nurse. I saw them exchange a look that I didn't understand.

He then turned back to me and frowned, his eyes filled with sadness. "You don't remember me?"

I studied his face and thought about it. "No, I don't think so," I finally said as I shook my head.

"What's the last thing you remember?" he asked me tentatively. I didn't need to know this man to detect the anxious expression on his face.

I stared at him and tried to rack my brain, searching for anything I could remember. I shook my head in frustration as I buried it in my hands. My head was pounding in pain as if I had just awoken from the worst hangover of my life.

"Liv, are you okay? What's wrong?" The alarm in his voice exacerbated the panic that was building inside.

"Why do you keep calling me Liv?" I felt annoyed as I looked back up at him. My annoyance turned to worry when I saw the shocked expression on his face.

The nurse stepped forward. "Do you remember your name?"

I opened my mouth, ready to answer her simple question, but then stopped. It was only then, when I was forced to think about it, that it dawned on me that I didn't actually know the answer. "I...I can't remember."

"Is there anything you do remember?" Her tone was gentle and cautious.

I searched my thoughts, trying to grab onto any memory. But everything outside the last few minutes seemed like a dream that I had somehow forgotten the moment I woke up. *Why can't I remember anything?* I shook my head in frustration. "What happened to me?"

"I'll let Mr. Brady here tell you what happened while I go get Dr. Miller."

"Honey, I'm Connor. Connor Brady. Are you sure you don't remember me?" The man moved back toward me, a mixture of hopefulness and uncertainty painted across his face.

"Connor," I repeated in a monotone voice. I studied him, trying to place him to some moment in my life. There was something about him that was familiar, but as hard as I tried, I couldn't seem to remember how I knew him. I shook my head slowly. "I don't even remember my own name."

"Your name is Olivia Stuart. Your friends call you Liv." He sat down on the chair next to my bed and placed his hand on top of mine. His hand was warm and familiar but it felt weird to have this stranger touching me in this intimate way. I didn't pull my hand away, though. I needed answers and this man seemed to have them, so the last thing I wanted to do was to offend him.

"What happened to me?"

His face fell. "You were in a hit-and-run accident." His voice cracked and he cleared his throat. He paused before continuing. "You've been in a coma for the past eight days since the accident."

Panic and confusion swirled around me at the idea of losing so much time without knowing it. "Eight days? But…but I don't remember any of this. Why can't I remember anything?" I felt frantic as I tried to push through the fog and my mind came back blank.

"Liv, you sustained some head injuries from the accident. The doctors said that memory loss was a possibility when you woke up…"

I stared at him in disbelief as my hands immediately moved up to my head. When my fingers traced the layers of bandages, I knew he was telling me the truth.

"Don't worry. The doctors say that if there's memory loss, it might only be temporary," he tried to reassure me. "You might slowly regain your memories back."

"Might?" I didn't feel reassured by that word.

Just then a middle-aged bald man in a white lab coat walked into the room. A warm smile appeared on his friendly face. "Ms. Stuart. I'm Dr. Miller. It's great to see you awake. How are you feeling?"

"What's wrong with me, Dr. Miller? Why can't I remember who I am?"

"Let me ask you a few questions first, alright?"

"Okay."

"Do you know when you were born?"

I searched my mind, trying to recall the answer. Nothing. I shook my head.

"Do you know where you went to high school?"

"No." I shook my head again as I felt the frustration and helplessness grow inside.

"Do you know the name of Philadelphia's football team?"

To my surprise, I didn't draw a blank this time. "The Eagles."

"You remember," Connor said excitedly as he squeezed my hand.

Dr. Miller smiled. "Can you tell me how many states there are in the U.S.?"

"Fifty." I frowned at the doctor, wondering if that was a trick question. "There are a few territories like Puerto Rico and Guam though," I added.

"Well, it looks like you've suffered from some memory loss due to the accident, but not all. It's not uncommon for someone to have some degree of amnesia after a traumatic event like the one you experienced. From your answers, it appears the amnesia has affected your episodic memory, which is the memory of experiences and specific events—the memories personal to you. But it seems that the amnesia didn't affect your semantic memory, which is the memory dealing with facts and your knowledge of the eternal world." He studied the clipboard in his hands. "The good news is from all the tests we've run on you, it doesn't seem like there was any damage to the areas of your brain that store your long-term memories."

"What does that mean, doctor?" the handsome man in the charcoal suit cut in to ask.

"Well it should mean that Ms. Stuart hasn't suffered any long-term memory loss."

"So I don't understand. Why can't I remember anything about myself, then?"

"That's the thing we don't know at this time. The brain is a miraculous and mysterious thing. It's unlikely that you're suffering from any permanent brain damage."

"So what's the problem?" Connor asked, his grip tightened around my hand.

"Sometimes the brain will suppress memories after going through a traumatic experience. That memory hasn't been forgotten in the traditional sense, but it's locked away by the sub-conscious and removed from the conscious mind."

"So does that mean I'll get my memories back?" I looked at him hopefully.

"The chances are good, but it's also not a guarantee either that you'll get some or all of your memories back. The best thing for you is to go back to your life before the accident and surround yourself with the things that are familiar and important to you—those are usually the things that will help trigger your memories."

"Liv, baby, I promise to help you through this." Connor held up my hand between both of his as he pulled it close to his chest. He looked up at Dr. Miller. "Doc, what's the next step?"

"Well Ms. Stuart, since you just woke up from the coma, I'd like to run some tests and keep you under careful observation at the hospital for a week or so. During this time, you'll also start your physical therapy to strengthen your muscles that have been inactive while you've been here. If the tests look good, then we can have you released as early as next week."

"Thank you, doctor. That's good news." Connor beamed at me.

But as much as I tried, I couldn't seem to adopt his excitement.

Sensing my unease, his expression changed. "What's wrong, honey?"

As if taking this as a signal, the doctor cleared his throat. "Ms. Stuart, we'll let you guys talk. I'll check up on you in an hour or so to run those tests."

Anxiety built inside me as I watched the doctor and nurse slip out of the room. Even though I knew that this man in the charcoal suit seemed to know who I was, he still felt like a stranger to me, and being completely alone with him made me uneasy.

"What are you thinking, Liv?" he finally broke the silence.

"Liv…Olivia." I said my name aloud. It sounded foreign, yet familiar from my mouth. I then met Connor's gaze. He smiled at me as he studied my expression. "I still don't know who you are exactly. I mean, I know your name is Connor, but…how do we know each other?"

His smile disappeared and I saw the sadness in his eyes again. "Liv, I'm your fiancé."

"Fiancé?"

He nodded. I followed his gaze as it darted down to my left hand. To my surprise, there on my ring finger was a large, sparkling diamond set on top of a platinum, diamond-encrusted eternity band. *How did I not see this earlier?*

I looked back at him in silence, overwhelmed by everything.

"This must be a lot for you to take in right now. And I'm sure you have a lot of questions. I'll be happy to answer whatever I know. Let's just take this one step at a time. We can go at the pace you're most comfortable with, okay?"

I nodded and drew in a deep breath as thousands of questions whirled around in my head, fighting for my attention.

"Thanks." I gave him a small smile, grateful for his patience and understanding. At that moment I thought about how hard this must be for him as well—to be engaged to and in love with someone who doesn't remember you or feel that same love anymore.

"Can we take this slowly? I just feel really overwhelmed."

"Of course, Liv. I understand. Whatever you need. Just tell me what you want. Okay?"

I nodded again. "Who are my parents? Do I have any siblings? Do they know I'm here?"

I saw the pained expression on Connor's face and knew I wouldn't like the answer.

"I'm sorry, Liv. Your mom passed away a few years ago. You don't have any siblings."

"Did you know my mom? What kind of person was she?" Tears streamed down my face as I felt the loss for the mother I couldn't remember.

"She passed away right before we met here in Philly. I believe you left New Jersey and moved here to start a new life."

"Oh. And my dad?"

He shook his head. "You rarely talked about him. From the little you have said, you haven't seen him since you were thirteen—"

"—when my parents got a divorce…" I finished his comment as I remembered the flashback I had right before I woke up.

"Yeah." Connor looked at me in alarm. "Are you remembering things?"

"Maybe. I had a flashback of them fighting when I was young right before I woke up."

"Oh. Did you get any other flashbacks?"

"I don't know. I think a little bit from the accident."

"Oh?"

"Yeah. I think I was running across the street and then a car came toward me and hit me."

"I'm so sorry, Liv." Connor buried his face in his hands. "It's all my fault."

"What do you mean? Were you driving that car?" I looked at him in alarm.

"No, of course not!" He shook his head. "I…I just feel responsible for you."

I frowned. I could tell there was something he wasn't telling me. "Do you know how my accident happened? Were you there?"

He nodded and looked away. "I wish I could take it all back. I wish…"

"What happened? Please tell me."

He looked up at me and I saw the regret in his face. "It was the night of our engagement party at the Franklin Institute Science Museum." His eyes glazed over and he smiled as his thoughts took him back to that night. "You looked absolutely gorgeous in that jeweled gown." He paused and his expression turned somber. "At some point during the night, you went out to the front of the museum. That's when the car hit you."

"I remember running across the street when the car hit me," I said slowly as I thought back to the flashback I had right before I woke up. I stared at him, trying to remember more from that night. *How come it's so hard to remember?* I thought in frustration.

"I'm so sorry, Liv. I should have been there for you. Maybe if I were there, this wouldn't have happened…"

I frowned, trying to figure out how to comfort this man who seemed to be consumed with guilt. "You didn't know this was going to happen." I saw the anguish in his eyes and reached for his hand to reassure him. "It's not your fault."

"But it did happen." I saw his body stiffen and knew it wasn't going to be easy for him to forgive himself.

"Connor, please don't."

He looked up at me with pained eyes.

"There's nothing you could've done differently when you didn't know. I wish I had my memories. I wish I hadn't been running across the street when the car came. I wish things were different." I blinked away a tear. "But sometimes we don't always get what we wish for. Sometimes we can only work with the hand that we're dealt." I was surprised by the sudden acceptance I felt for what had happened. *Maybe those who say, "ignorance is bliss," are right.*

"Is there anything I can do to help?"

I looked at this stranger and somehow I knew I would remember him again. I knew he was important to me. I looked down at the engagement ring on my finger and instantly felt a loss for all the special memories that I didn't have anymore.

"What's wrong, Liv?" He saw the fresh tears in my eyes that were threatening to make their way down my cheeks.

"It's just a lot to take in all at once."

"I know."

I watched him gently brush the tears from my cheeks, and from the way his hands caressed my face, I knew he'd touched me many times before. *Were we happy before this accident? What kind of person was I when we were together? What did I enjoy doing?* It wasn't until then that another question hit me like a ton of bricks. *What do I look like?*

I gave him a weak smile. "Connor, I'm really tired. I'd like some time alone to digest all this."

His brows furrowed with worry but he didn't try to object. "Okay." He got up from the chair and looked down at me. "I'll stop by first thing tomorrow morning to see you."

"Okay." I forced a small smile.

He leaned down toward me and kissed me gently on my forehead. "I'll see you tomorrow. I love you, gorgeous," he whispered.

As I watched him leave, the hospital room suddenly disappeared.

For a split second I found myself in a grand, sun-drenched bedroom lying naked on a large luxurious bed under lush layers of satin sheets. I screamed out and my back arched upward as intense pleasure radiated throughout my body. I felt a pair of strong, rough hands grip my thighs tightly, keeping them spread apart as a long and hard tongue plunged in and out of me, pushing me to the brink of my release. After I came, I felt another naked body move up my body from somewhere under the layers and a second later, Connor's face emerged out from under the sheets. He flashed me a wicked smirk as he slowly licked his lips. "And that's how much I love you, gorgeous."

I gasped at the memory that had just hit me, and my body tingled as if that moment had just happened. I looked down at my body and the question that had blindsided me a few minutes earlier crossed my mind again. *What do I look like?*

I slowly got up from the bed, and felt my muscles weak from the days of being on the hospital bed. It took me several minutes to move to the bathroom where there was a full-length mirror along the wall facing the door.

Standing in front of the mirror was like standing face to face with a complete stranger. Nerves prickled through my body like ice, cold needles as I studied every inch of the unfamiliar person in front of me. Nothing about my reflection looked familiar. Her radiant blue eyes stared back at me. Even through the bandages around her forehead, I could see the long wavy blond hair that cascaded down the curves of her small frame. I watched as this stunning woman staring back at me touched her face with both hands. I felt her fingers move across my face.

"I'm Olivia Stuart." My whispered words filled the silent room and seemed to hang in the air as I continued to study myself in the reflection. *Will this ever stop feeling so strange?*

***

After a week at the hospital and focusing on my physical therapy, I felt slightly better and hopeful about everything. The tests Dr. Miller had ran all came out normal and I was cleared to leave today.

"Hey, gorgeous."

I looked up to find Connor at my door with a large bouquet of pink roses.

"Hi." I smiled, happy to see a familiar face. "You're back."

"Of course I'm back, silly. I've been visiting you every day, and every day you seem surprised to see me. Are you trying to get rid of me or something?"

I could see from his smile that he was joking, and I giggled uneasily. "No, that's not what I mean." I wasn't sure how to tell him that the reason I seemed surprised to see him was because to me, he felt like a stranger.

"Well, like it or not, I'm here to take you home today, like I'd promised."

"Oh, right." Our eyes met and I felt my stomach flip nervously. I immediately looked away and felt my face turn beet red when I remembered my flashback of the intense orgasm this man had given me. I knew that for him, we were lovers in love, but for me, I felt embarrassed and exposed that this handsome stranger knew me more intimately than I knew myself.

"What's wrong?" He walked over to me and kissed me lightly on my cheek.

"Nothing." I pushed my thoughts aside and flashed him a smile.

He handed me the bouquet in his hands. "Pink roses are your favorite."

"Thank you. They're beautiful." I took the stunning bouquet and was instantly hit with its intoxicating smell.

"How are you feeling?"

"Better," I responded honestly.

"Good. So are you ready to blow this popsicle stand then?"

I let out a light chuckle and nodded.

Thirty minutes later, Connor had helped me finish all my paperwork to check out of the hospital. I had changed into a white Splendid cotton silk tee, dark-washed J Brand jeans, and a pair of black Christian Louboutin patent leather stilettos that Connor brought for me from my closet. According to him, this was one of my favorite casual outfits. I had stared dubiously at the three-inch heels when he had handed them to me. They looked more painful than comfortable to me. But when I put them on, they had hugged my feet perfectly and I was surprised by how at ease I was walking around in them.

"Hey, gorgeous." Connor looked up from the hospital paperwork when I walked out of the bathroom. "You look like you're back to your old self." I watched as his eyes moved up and down my body, and a nervous shiver ran down my back.

"I guess my muscle memory's still intact," I joked as I looked at my heels.

He chuckled and shook his head. "I never did understand how you could walk in those things. You know on one of our first dates, I called you Wonder Woman when I saw you running in a pair just like those."

I smiled. "Why was I running?"

"We had just had an amazing date at Tria, this great wine bar in the city, and you had a few glasses too many." He smiled as he told the story. "Well, by the end of the night, you were running and skipping down the street without a care in the world and giggling uncontrollably." He laughed at the memory and beamed at me. "It was at that moment that I knew I'd fall in love with you."

I laughed along with him, wishing I could remember that memory, wishing I could remember how it had felt to possibly share those same feelings toward him.

A few minutes later we were outside, standing at the entrance of the hospital.

"Liv, I'm going to go get the car. You okay with waiting right here for me? I'll bring the car around and pick you up."

I nodded and smiled. He's such a gentleman.

He leaned in and kissed me gently on the forehead. "I love you, gorgeous."

"Thanks." I cringed inside as soon as the word came out. I wasn't sure what to say. I had a feeling he wanted more, but telling a stranger I loved him wasn't something I was ready to give.

He gave a light chuckle and smiled. "I'll be back."

As I watched him walk away and turn the corner toward the entrance of the parking garage, I was preoccupied with thoughts of how the following days, weeks, and months would be for us.

Suddenly I heard people approach me from the left.

"Excuse me! Please make way!"

I turned and saw a couple barreling toward me. It was a man holding up a pregnant woman who appeared to be in a lot of pain. "My wife's water broke! Please move!"

I finally realized that I was standing in the middle of the hospital entrance and blocking their path. I hastily took a step back to give them room to pass me, but it was too late. The man pushed past me and as I took a step back, my heel caught on a crack in the pavement and I lost my balance and fell backward.

Just as I thought I was about to hit the ground, a strong arm caught me from behind and pulled me up. I gasped in surprise at my near-fall and found myself tightly clutched within someone's protective arms.

"Careful there or you're going to hurt yourself in those killer heels."

I looked up and let out an audible gasp as my gaze locked with a pair of intensely-dark, smoldering brown eyes staring down at me.

If you enjoyed this excerpt from *Oblivion*, a completely standalone full-length book, the book is currently available.

About the Author

Jessica Wood writes new adult contemporary romance.

While she has lived in countless cities throughout the U.S., her heart belongs to San Francisco. To her, there's something seductively romantic about the Golden Gate Bridge, the steep rolling hills of the city streets, the cable cars, and the Victorian-style architecture.

Jessica loves a strong, masculine man with a witty personality. While she is headstrong and stubbornly independent, she can't resist a man who takes control of the relationship, both outside and inside of the bedroom.

She loves to travel internationally, and tries to plan a yearly trip abroad. She also loves to cook and bake, and—to the benefit of her friends—she loves to share. She also enjoys ceramics and being creative with her hands. She has a weakness for good (maybe bad) TV shows; she's up-to-date on over 25 current shows, and no, that wasn't a joke.

And it goes without saying, she loves books—they're like old and dear friends who have always been there to make her laugh and make her cry.

The one thing she wished she had more of is time.

If you would like to follow or contact Jessica Wood, you can do so through the following:

Mailing List: http://jessicawoodauthor.com/mailing-list/

Blog: http://jessicawoodauthor.com

Facebook: www.facebook.com/jessicawoodauthor

Twitter: http://twitter.com/jesswoodauthor

Pinterest: http://pinterest.com/jessicawooda/